The Rain Will Tell

Myra Towner-Rankin

A gripping debut, you don't want to miss!

- DELIA C., Author of *Fallin' Out*

Copyright © 2004 by Myra Rankin

ISBN 0-7414-2020-2

Edited by Jane Loeb- New York

Jacket photo by: Broderick Maxwell

Published by:

INFI∞ITY
PUBLISHING.COM

1094 New DeHaven Street, Suite 100
West Conshohocken, PA 19428-2713
Info@buybooksontheweb.com
www.buybooksontheweb.com
Toll-free (877) BUY BOOK
Local Phone (610) 941-9999
Fax (610) 941-9959

Printed in the United States of America
Printed on Recycled Paper
Published February 2005

Acknowledgments

To My Daughter Brittany,
It has been said that "Raising A Teenager Is Like
Trying To Nail Jell-O To A Tree."
I say, the success all depends on how well it is molded.
Keep making me proud, my little Booska!

Many Kind Thanks To:
My Sister Mert, who truly is my "other half";
My Mom, Anna Mae, who believes in me;
My Brother C.J., who always asks, "Hey, how is that
book coming?"
My niece Angela, who is my little Miracle and my
biggest fan;
Barry, who is always looking out for me;
Dee, who has helped me realize that we can "Walk
Through It"
And especially to God, who put all these special
people in my life.

My Prayer:
Lord, before you open the gates of Heaven and tell me
it's my time,
Please let me see the words of my first novel bound
between a spine.

*I Can Do All Things Through Christ Which
Strengtheneth me.*
(PHILIPPIANS 4:13)

Prologue

Both of JoVonna's parents end up dead within months of each other, and she knows who is responsible. She has a plan to avenge the death of her parents, even though the guilty person is already dead. A very lucrative business deal between JoVonna's father and the former Mayor, Virgil Billford, resulted in JoVonna's father walking away from the deal with an enormous amount of money, while the former mayor received a pittance. From his grave, Virgil turns the town upside down, leaving stipulations in his Will that lead to lies, fierce competition, sex, theft, tears, cheers and murder.

JoVonna solicits help from the current Mayor, Marcus Brackner, offering him "anything" if he can undo what the former mayor has done and restore her family's reputation. Marcus can't help her. Virgil leaves a Will with instructions that won't allow the changes JoVonna is seeking. Still, Marcus does not want to take on JoVonna as an enemy, not with his re-election coming up. This Grand Lady is much too powerful. Money, her father's business savvy, and revenge for the death of her parents are just a few of the weapons in her arsenal.

Collectively, the residents of the town of Richland Hills, Mississippi have fought, blackmailed, lied, bribed, hired hate groups, lusted, prayed and put the entire matter in the hands of a greater power. Trained killers descended upon the town. Their victim believed the reason they gave for being in her home in the middle of the night. They had drinks and completed a business deal– one that she would never remember.

Mayor Marcus Brackner has committed a horrible sin,......... or did he? Will the Christmas present he gives Lilly prove his innocence to her and the entire town? What will it take to make her open it?

Margot has been a housekeeper and personal assistant to JoVonna for years. She uses what she has learned to secure a future that includes the finer things of life– on her own terms. JoVonna finds some disturbing items in Margot's room. Are these items harmless, or does she pose a threat to her boss?

Deception is merged into the media and a key player must now attempt to pay members of the City Council, as well as a perfect stranger, for information on the segment of her life that elapsed while she was comatose; otherwise, she'll never know who fathered her child. This child ends up in the hands of the very people she has watched through binoculars and feared, yet found the courage to intimidate. The Grand Jury has to determine if it will indict the Grand Lady. At least, that's what her status used to be, in this small town in Mississippi, where the torrential rains have destroyed footprints and a briefcase full of documents on its way to court. Will the Court or someone else decide the Grand Lady's fate?.......THE RAIN WILL TELL.

THE RAIN WILL TELL

Chapter One

Richland Hills, Mississippi 1958

The Mayor of Richland Hills made his way through the crowd to compliment the hostess.

"This is an exquisite party, JoVonna."

"Thank you Mayor Brackner, but you know as well as I, that I put my best efforts into my endeavors. As they say in business, 'good results don't just happen.' I have been intending to host a dinner party for you for some time. Unfortunately, my calendar would not permit it until now."

She looked at him with her head slightly lowered and her eyes pointed upward like an apologetic schoolgirl. The mayor smiled as he turned and walked away. JoVonna's hands caressed the pure silk, teal-colored dress she wore as she allowed her thoughts to aimlessly drift, remembering as she handed the check for three thousand dollars to Raphael, her dressmaker, how he had jokingly admonished her not to make any sudden moves. This thought brought a smile to her face and she made a mental note to send Raphael something befitting his outrageous personality for his upcoming birthday.

JoVonna continued to daydream as she walked out into her beautifully manicured gardens, appointed with fragrant honeysuckle, fiery red azaleas, camellias and southern magnolia trees whose blossoms fell from the trees and pirouetted to the ground like tiny ballet dancers. There were also apple blossoms and four kinds of breath-taking roses blooming in defiance of the unseasonably cool weather. JoVonna's parents had helped to plant most of these flowers and trees, and used to enjoy countless hours sitting out in the garden. The garden reminded her of the kind of relationship her parents had. Her father had been strong and unwavering like the mature oak trees that made zigzagging patterns across her property. Her mother was beautiful but her health had always been very delicate. JoVonna looked at the wilting potted plant in front of her and sighed. JoVonna's home, which was richly appointed in silks, jade, leather and other keepsakes, left nothing to be desired materialistically. It radiated wealth, and the thought of the people that lived less than an acre and one half from her sent her blood rushing. She glanced down at her garage. Her Mediterranean-blue Mercedes and her prized Silver Shadow Rolls Royce were still in tact. The Cadillac that was used to run errands sat in front of the garage. She had never actually talked to any of *those people,* but she had heard plenty of rumors, and it was no telling what they were capable of. She didn't know anything about the kind of people that now occupied the property so close to hers, but she did know that her father had been blamed for them being there and that practically the entire town turned against her family. In her mind, those people were the reason both of her parents were dead.

JoVonna despised the fact that the former mayor of Richland Hills, Mississippi, a community even more affluent than Montgomery County, Maryland, had demanded in his Will that those undeserving land leeches should each have land that just was not meant for them. The thought of this situation and what she had to do about it set JoVonna back in tune with her mission. She rushed back into the party just as some of her invited guests, which consisted of attorneys, land surveyors, commissioners, business owners and city councilmen began gathering minks, blue foxes and other assorted furs for their spouses or companions.

JoVonna walked past Margot, her assistant and housekeeper, who was busying herself making sure there was an abundance of caviar and other imported delicacies for the remaining guests. The overall spirit of those gathered was radiant as a result of the continuously flowing champagne fountains positioned at each end of the serving table.

2

JoVonna caught a glimpse of herself in the mirrored wall from across the room. What she saw was a sophisticated, sexy and business savvy young woman. Almost anyone else looking at that same reflection would have seen a cold-hearted and calculating bitch who used people up and then kept them around to remind them that they were nothing. Margot was far too busy to notice her employer watching her. She moved back and forth, coordinating the cooks, servers and bartenders, and at her direction, the dinner party was progressing flawlessly. As she continued to watch, JoVonna admitted to herself that Margot had the potential to be an effective and prominent business woman, but she lacked the one thing it took to have any significant influence in this town, or even in this room, and that was money, and lots of it. Margot had accepted the offer to become JoVonna's assistant because she was young and just happened to be in a very difficult situation when the two of them met, but JoVonna knew that Margot was both intelligent and beautiful. She shook off the thought and moved through the crowd to catch Marcus before he left. "Mayor, I haven't seen your– what's her name all evening. Are you alone?"

"Yes. Lilly is away on business."

She pondered that thought while nibbling on an olive and moved closer to make sure she had his undivided attention.

"Would it be possible to see you for just a moment after the rest of my guests have gone?"

The mayor looked at JoVonna over his champagne glass and said, "Certainly, I believe I have five or ten minutes."

JoVonna moved even closer to him and said," What I want to discuss will certainly take longer than five or ten minutes." She tilted her head and let her hair cascade down her back as she laughed and turned to walk away. The mayor, whose alcohol level was making the decisions for him on this evening, followed the dress, the walk and the

3

perfume across the room with his eyes. He draped his suit coat over a large leather chair that sat next to the floor-to-ceiling fireplace.

As the last of her guests began to say goodnight, JoVonna air kissed each of her female guests and offered warm and friendly hugs to some of the gentlemen. She also sized up each of the men and women as they left for how they could benefit her cause– to eliminate those awful people who, in her opinion, did not deserve to live in Richland Hills. When she finally closed the heavy double doors for the evening, JoVonna was excited about being alone with the mayor to try and persuade him to her point of view.

She spoke to Margot, who was already inspecting the results of the dinner party and instructing the hired help on what had to be done before they left for the evening. "Margot, you can have the rest of the evening to yourself, but make sure the help understands that this mess has to be cleared first."

JoVonna took the Mayor into her study to ensure privacy, and began by picking very choice words to reiterate her position while trying to be persuasive without being authoritative, which was very difficult for her. She asked the mayor to try to envision the time a few years ago when old money changed hands from generation to generation and persons not measuring up to a certain stature were not even allowed in this community.

JoVonna continued to talk while watching his reaction. She crossed her legs and smoothed her dress. He watched. She dropped the napkin that surrounded her martini glass and leaned over to retrieve it. The neckline of the dress offered Marcus a generous view of her breasts, and he did not avert his eyes. When she sensed that the effect of the drinks, combined with the mayor's curiosity about her had peaked, JoVonna walked over to the chair where he was seated and sat astride him, causing the seams of her dress to protest as it was elevated to expose silky thighs. She loosened his tie and began slowly kissing his eyelids and when he found it difficult to sit still, JoVonna responded to his advances and gestures with a passionate kiss.

"Marcus."

"Yes?" Marcus' answer was muffled as he kissed the ample breasts that strained against the neckline of her dress.

"I want you to use every ounce of clout you have to find a way for me to purchase that land those people live on and have those unsightly eyesores they call homes torn down so that we can restore this community to what it once was."

Marcus leaned back in the chair and sighed. He thought about the stack of correspondence she had sent to his office on that very same subject.

"JoVonna, I am acquainted with several of the best lawyers money can buy. I am also affiliated with some very influential and successful organizations, but even with that kind of support behind you, you cannot just force law abiding, tax-paying people to sell their land to you if they choose not to. There are no roads or city improvements scheduled to come through their land, nor is there any reason for the city to condemn it."

"Are you saying that there is nothing you can do to make them sell to me? That land belongs to my family!"

"Yes. That is what I am saying, JoVonna." You should try to be reasonable."

JoVonna removed her hand, which had found its way inside the mayor's unzipped trousers and zipped them up so quickly that he grimaced in pain and stood as he tried desperately to separate his flesh from the zipper that now held him hostage. JoVonna backed up and stood facing him.

"Get out of my home!" she shouted. "If you cannot find it within your means to get my family's land back, then you certainly don't deserve anything I can offer you."

He took several deep breaths to allow the pain to subside, and when he could speak again, he tried to reason with her.

"JoVonna, they own that land and- "

"Get out!"

The mayor gritted his teeth to offset the pain in his pants and drove home with the thought of the beautiful, yet vindictive woman he had just left and wondered what he had almost gotten himself into. He did not want to take her on as an enemy. She was much too powerful for that. He vowed to call her at her office the next day to try to reason with her again.

THE RAIN WILL TELL
Chapter Two

"Margot, where are you? I need you to help me find my eel-skinned shoes, and I asked you to take my jewelry to be polished some time ago, so make damned sure it's done before I get home from the office this evening. And another thing, place an order with the butcher for filet mignon and instruct him to steam two lobster tails for me. You can pick the order up after you finish the list of things I left for you to do. If I decide to have a guest this evening, I want dinner served promptly at six o'clock, so don't make any personal plans."

Margot walked slowly down the hall as JoVonna's orders rang out towards her. The two women were almost exactly the same height and eyed each other momentarily as JoVonna turned to pick up her briefcase off the marble counter that separated her breakfast nook from the kitchen. JoVonna secretly envied Margot for the fact that she had come to her home with nothing, but acted as if she would know exactly how to run the world if it were at her disposal. She consoled herself as she started her Mercedes with the thought that of all the housekeepers she had employed, Margot was the best. Margot did just exactly what JoVonna told her and this was something JoVonna had become very accustomed to. She would simply accept nothing less.

The drive to her office which was located in the prestigious Waltham Towers was no less tedious than any other, and on this day, the magnificent tree-lined streets and the meticulously manicured flowers and shrubs at every median temporarily distracted JoVonna's thoughts. A pair of butterflies out for a morning ride on the wind rested on a rose bush.

This is a beautiful community, and those people just don't belong here. JoVonna thought to herself. As she continued driving to her office, JoVonna remembered when

Virgil Parker had served as the mayor of Richland Hills. During that time, he purchased ten acres of land from her father, who owned a great deal of land and nearly every prosperous business in the entire community. The land was immediately adjacent to the acreage that JoVonna's father had built a mansion on and given to her as a birthday present.

Shortly after, a business agreement between her father and Mayor Virgil Parker plummeted. When the agreement resulted in the mayor losing several million dollars while JoVonna's father made a vast profit, the two men became bitter enemies.

Mayor Virgil Parker blamed JoVonna's father for telling vicious lies aimed at ruining his character and turning the town against him. When he lost his bid for a second term in office, Virgil swore that JoVonna's father was to blame and threatened that the "High and Mighty" Rossier name would be dragged through the mud before he was finished.

After Marcus Brackner was sworn in as the new mayor, Virgil Parker was discretely persuaded to leave Richland Hills. He blamed JoVonna's father for this as well and still refused to sell the ten acres of land he had purchased years ago to anyone. On the day he was scheduled to leave town, he was admitted to the Richland Hills Community Hospital. Two hours later, he was pronounced dead of a massive heart attack.

At the reading of Virgil's Will, the entire community was shocked to learn that the former mayor's Will stipulated that ten families from Greenspoint, Mississippi, a community that still used outhouses and survived in clapboard shacks, would inherit the property right next to JoVonna's. They would be situated on some of the best land in Richland Hills. The Will further stipulated that funds from a bank account the now deceased former mayor had left active in Georgia when he relocated to Mississippi would be used to build each family a modest two-bedroom house. The remainder of the money would be used to pay taxes on the property and the homes for the next several years. The Will directed that

8

additional funds would be used to retain a very prominent attorney licensed to practice in Mississippi and South Carolina as on-going counsel for the families and left them several mature bonds as well. Virgil Parker had selected the families himself and listed their names in his Will. The families were notified of Virgil's intentions and told that they should hire their own construction crews. They were very afraid of what was being offered to them. They wondered why a white man in Mississippi would give them homes and land and pay the taxes on it while in the next town, some of their neighbors were randomly being burned out of theirs. They refused to have anything to do with the property until their lawyer repeatedly assured them that this was now their land and that the property deeds gave them every right to live there. They moved their meager possessions in battered station wagons and trucks in the middle of the night, and then set up shifts to watch all night. JoVonna began spending money doing things that she thought would make them turn and run the day they moved in. The cross burnings she paid for continued until the families no longer hid in their houses, but instead gathered together the morning after the fires to read their Bibles and pray at the site of the burned crosses.

JoVonna's father was killed in an automobile accident soon afterwards. She hired her own investigator and together, they labored over every scrap of evidence, but the reason for the brakes failing in a brand new Cadillac was never determined. JoVonna's mother had always been fragile. She was noticeably shaken by her husband's death and the wrath of living hell that was descended upon her by the community as result of her husband's business deals and what he had, in their opinion, allowed to happen to their community. Her mother became ill and was confined to her bed. Within a very short time, JoVonna had lost both her parents and found new comfort in a bottle of liquor. JoVonna had no other relatives. She was determined to restore her family's name and get rid of those freeloaders who, in her opinion, had caused her family such misery. From that point, she set out in a desperate effort to make sure she knew where all of her father's other land was, who was renting it and whether there were any pending deals for land to be sold.

JoVonna's thoughts turned back to the situation at hand as she wheeled her Mercedes into the parking space reserved for her just outside the front door of the Waltham Towers. She thought about all the work waiting on her desk and wished she had gotten to the office earlier. She noticed how exquisitely the Magnolias bloomed in the huge granite pots that lined the entrance way to Waltham Towers and again thought to herself that a community this beautiful should have no blemishes. Just inside the door, Miss Toliver, the receptionist, greeted her and as they said good morning, JoVonna paused momentarily to inspect her suit in the spotless, polished brass doors just ahead of her. She took the elevator to the top floor, rearranging her hair as she looked in the glass walls of the elevator. The white silk suit she wore complimented her figure as well as her complexion and JoVonna felt up to whatever tasks were behind the doors of her office.

THE RAIN WILL TELL

Chapter Three

JoVonna entered the small reception area adjacent to her office where her new Office Administrator sat. Shirley had only been employed at Rossier Industries for a short while but she already knew how difficult it could be to work for JoVonna. Still, it couldn't be any worse than the last job she had where her boss forced himself on her in his office. She knew the police would never believe her story. After all, she was a Negro woman and he was a very prominent, white businessman. If she told her husband, he would have killed her boss and most certainly gone to prison or even worse, been executed, leaving her to raise four boys all alone. Her only recourse had been to find another job and she intended to keep this one. Shirley whirled around in her chair at the sound of the door opening so suddenly.

"Good morning, Miss Rossier." Shirley said as she simultaneously reached into her desk drawer for some aspirin.

"It will be a good morning if I have anything to do with it" JoVonna retorted. Just outside the door bearing the letters (J. Rossier) etched in gold, JoVonna turned to Shirley and said," Mix a martini for me, bring in my messages and cancel all appointments until after noon."

"But it's only 9:30 and -"

"I am perfectly capable of keeping track of time as well as the salary I pay you to do exactly what I tell you without question. Is that explicit enough for you or should I employ a service to fill your seat right now?"

"I'll bring in the things you asked for immediately." Shirley replied. She put a memo from Timothy Wells, the vice president of Rossier Industries on top of the stack. *JoVonna Rossier easily has two professions. First and foremost, Occupational Bitch, secondly, CEO to the hugely*

11

successful Conglomerate, Rossier Industries. Shirley thought. She wondered why JoVonna worked at all, why she did not simply sell her companies, take the profit she would net in the sales and add that to the incredible sum of very old money she inherited when her parents died. JoVonna worked for the power, the knowledge that she was, and would always be in control. JoVonna crushed people. Shirley knocked on JoVonna's door and opened it slightly. JoVonna motioned to her to come in. Shirley busied herself making the drink and sat it down in JoVonna's coaster. She put JoVonna's messages, which were always, at JoVonna's request, in sequence by time of call and then alphabetized, on her desk. Shirley witnessed JoVonna engrossed in a full-blown heated discussion with a very unfortunate party on the other end of the line about appraisal values and a disgrace to the community of Richland Hills. JoVonna called whomever she was speaking with a damned egalitarian and slammed the receiver down.

After Shirley had gone, JoVonna picked up the crystal glass and consumed over half its contents before replacing it in the hand-carved wooden coaster that always sat on her desk. JoVonna took a deep breath and looked around her office. In the center of the office sat her oversized rosewood desk. On one side of the desk was JoVonna's leather high-backed chair. Positioned on the other side of the desk were two smaller leather chairs of the same lavish quality. To her right was an oak wood conference table with six chairs positioned on each side and water pitchers at each end. Immediately behind the conference table were six bookshelves that consisted of what amounted to her own personal library. To her left was an aquarium with exotic species of fish and in the corner, a built-in, fully stocked wet bar with Gin and Vodka being the beverages of choice. The sparse wall space in the office was appointed with paintings that were expensive, even to the untrained eye. The exterior of Waltham Towers was almost exclusively glass, which afforded JoVonna a breathtaking view of the historical district of the central region of Mississippi.

JoVonna had just finished her drink when the telephone rang. She picked up the receiver.

"JoVonna?"

"Yes."

"This is Mayor—it's Marcus Brackner. I have been giving some thought to your predicament–you know–with your neighbors and all, and I am not going to be able to help you."

"Mayor, you didn't have to call me to repeat the crap you told me last night. If you had any clout, you would have used it by now. Two things are very obvious here: One, you are of no use or value to me, and two, I'm going to make sure you are painfully reminded of your lack of concern for me as a loyal political supporter when your term expires and you try to get re-elected. And by the way, about the Annual Mayor's Banquet, I suppose that since I have already paid the caterers and the orchestra, and given that I am the guest speaker, I will make an appearance, but I warn you, don't do anything else that might even vaguely irritate me. I will see to it that when your term expires that you are sweeping streets instead of going to dedication ceremonies to name them." JoVonna slammed the receiver back into its cradle and reached for her drink.

THE RAIN WILL TELL
Chapter Four

In the weeks that preceded the Annual Mayor's Banquet, JoVonna spent the majority of her time finding menial tasks to keep Margot away from the mansion so that she could take advantage of every opportunity to sit glaring through her binoculars, watching her unwanted neighbors. Margot and JoVonna argued on more than one occasion about JoVonna's obsession with watching her neighbors. Margot had long since grown weary of hearing JoVonna complain about them and their children with hair that was bad enough to be convicted of a crime all by itself. JoVonna complained about the clothes they wore and how the men surely must have served hard time in some prison on a chain gang, because they had bodies that looked like smooth black armor.

For JoVonna, the list of things that made her unwelcome neighbors unacceptable never ended. She massaged her temples and released the gold barrette that held her hair almost motionless as she strode over to the bar to fix a drink. She turned towards her writing desk. The top drawer was slightly ajar. JoVonna walked over to the desk drawer. Inside was a stack of checks made payable to each of the ten families along with surveyor's reports and all of the other documents she had collected in her attempt to take land that she knew was not hers but wanted for her mother and father's sake.

JoVonna's temper flared momentarily as she remembered the Sunday morning when she looked through her binoculars and witnessed the women from each of the families gathered together in front of one of their homes. JoVonna had gotten dressed and driven her Mercedes the short distance to where the women congregated. She got out of her car and approached the women cautiously, not fully knowing what to expect, and certainly not wanting to be in too close contact with any member of this group of shiny black women in hideous straw hats that now stood before her. JoVonna cleared her throat and began to speak. "Take these checks. I have one for each family. There is enough here for you to purchase homes someplace else, closer to your own kind, so that I..uh..so that you can be more comfortable." JoVonna recalled that she felt angry and uncomfortable as the women formed a circle around her and began to sing a hymn with a chorus of "He Watches Over The Sparrow, And I Know He Watches Over Me." When the women finished the song, they all, almost simultaneously turned their backs to her and waited in silence for her to leave. JoVonna could not recall when she had been so humiliated or angry without someone at least losing his or her jobs as a result. A woman of her caliber, it seemed, would be helpless against this small group of people, at least for now. JoVonna was jolted back to the present by the sound of the telephone ringing.

"Hello."

"Vonna, darling, it's Raphael. I've created a sensational gown for your appearance at the Annual Mayor's Banquet. How soon can you be fitted?"

JoVonna took a long, slow sip of her martini and savored the taste of the olive until the last bite had been swallowed and replied, "I'll be there about noon tomorrow, and there is one other thing, Raphael."

"Yes, darling?"

"I pay you enough to call me by my name at all times, is that clearly understood?"

"Why certainly, 'Vonna.....uh, Ms. Rossier, it won't happen again."

JoVonna walked into her kitchen and took the tray of chilled shrimp that Margot prepared for her out of the refrigerator. She walked through the glass doors that led from her breakfast nook into her flower gardens and sat down while she systematically popped shrimp in her mouth.

JoVonna pondered whom she would choose next to engage in a tête-à-tête regarding removing those people from the community and restoring her family's good name. She would be relentless until she felt in her heart that wherever her parents were, they knew she had exhausted all avenues. JoVonna made a mental note of what she would have Margot order from the butcher for her meal selections for the upcoming week and drifted off to sleep.

THE RAIN WILL TELL
Chapter Five

The sudden onslaught of rain saturated JoVonna before she awakened completely. She jumped to her feet, upsetting the small table where she had placed the shrimp platter and a glass that contained a small amount of the martini that had destined her to such a sound sleep. Once inside, she stood watching the heavy downpour of rain nourishing her gardens. Her conscience momentarily allowed her to feel a sort of pity for the residents of Greenspoint and other small outlying areas of Mississippi that had no proper drainage or sewer systems. It rained very frequently throughout Mississippi, and as a result, water rose and remained so stagnant that the residents of Greenspoint could practically grow rice. The feeling of sympathy disappeared as quickly as it had come, and JoVonna turned to see Margot standing just inside the doorway to the kitchen.

"Margot, I'd like to have a couple of steaks and some fresh fish added to the list for the butcher, and give him the message that he better not dare send me anything that he's had for longer than one day."

"I'll add those things to the list right away. What vegetables do you want?" Margot asked over her shoulder. JoVonna had been drinking more heavily lately so Margot purposely did not ask if she wanted the bar restocked.

"I'll let you know later. Right now I need a hot bath."

As JoVonna left the room, she continued to call out instructions to Margot until the sound of her voice was no longer audible. Margot had to choose between straining to hear her or following her around the mansion.

"Get a cleaning service in here first thing tomorrow. I want this place cleaned from top to bottom. If you can't find a better service than you used last time, then you can clean this entire place yourself. Oh, and stop feeding that damned stray cat. I don't want it hanging around here any more." JoVonna slammed the door, leaving Margot standing there. She sank into the steaming hot tub of water and sighed. She had never even entertained the thought of allowing anyone except Margot to stay in the mansion with her on a regular basis. JoVonna cherished her privacy too much. She laughed at the irony that, except for her dinner parties and work-related events, she had a rather reclusive lifestyle, while at the same time, she always knew the comings and goings of her neighbors.

JoVonna dated infrequently and was very selective about which gentlemen occupied her time. The thought of marriage terrified her. She had watched her father make very important decisions that her mother rarely challenged and decided long ago that she would make her own decisions; she would decide what was best for her, and that was final. JoVonna's thoughts meandered until the combination of the tepid water and light tapping at the bathroom door caused her to get out of the tub. Margot had come to know when JoVonna wanted to be alone, so she left JoVonna's dinner and her drink on the table, set a dish of milk out for the orphaned cat and retired to her quarters for the evening. JoVonna finished her meal, took her drink to her library and reviewed some progress reports Shirley had given her as she left her office. Her library faced the land her neighbors owned, and when she finished what she brought home from the office, she reached for her binoculars and began her ritual of watching them until they retired for the evening. She made notes on her strategy to get them off of the land.

THE RAIN WILL TELL
Chapter Six

JoVonna walked through the reception area adjacent to her office. Shirley saw the expression on her face and reached in her drawer for her aspirin.

"Shirley, I am not taking any unscheduled appointments today. I want the minutes from the last Board Meeting on my desk in five minutes. Make copies of the list of possible future acquisitions for all the members of my leadership committee, get Timothy Wells on the telephone and schedule a staff meeting two weeks from today. I want lunch catered, and tell Mr. Simms if he wants to infringe on my valuable time, he better be here at 10:00 instead of 12:30. I've made other plans. I'll be leaving the office at 11:30 today."

As JoVonna walked into her office, she looked at the wet bar and then back at Shirley, issuing a silent command with her eyes. Shirley got up and began mixing the drink. JoVonna swore to herself as she remembered she had left her briefcase in her Mercedes and headed out of the office and back to her car. As she walked past Ms. Toliver at the receptionist desk, she was reminded of a telephone call she had received from one of her friends inquiring about a job for her daughter while she was home from college. When JoVonna returned to her office, she picked up the receiver and dialed the building manager.

"Good Morning, Mr. Morgan's office."

"Tell him it is JoVonna Rossier."

"One moment, please."

"JoVonna, What can I do for you?"

"Well, Bill, as you know, I have several customers and clients in and out of the building throughout the day, and quite frankly, I'm worried that Miss Toliver is a threat to the professional image we try to maintain here at Waltham

Towers. She's just not polished, if you know what I mean. She has misdirected clients to my office on more than one occasion. I have someone in mind that I know would fulfill the image we need in the main reception area."

Bill Morgan hesitated, thinking about what this favor for JoVonna might someday lead to. Sweat beaded up on his forehead. He loosened his tie.

"Well, we can interview her at 8:00 on Monday. Is there anything else I can do for you, JoVonna?"

"No. Thanks. We should have lunch again soon. Let my secretary know when would be a good day."

"Okay JoVonna. I will see you soon."

A smiled crossed JoVonna's lips. "Shirley, get Mrs. Crawford on the telephone and tell her that I managed to find a job opening in the building after all and that her daughter will start working here at 8:00 on Monday. Then, call Raphael and let him know that I will be there at about noon to be fitted for my dress. Tell him to clear out all of those tramps who should be buying off the rack, because I don't want to spend all day there and I want his time exclusively."

JoVonna turned and walked back into her office. Shirley had not seen any job openings posted and wondered what her boss was up to. As the door to JoVonna's office closed, Shirley's eyes bored a hole in her back. Later, as she walked down the hall and past Miss Toliver, JoVonna flashed a painted smiled and headed for her car to go see Raphael. She paused momentarily to take in the aroma of the fresh flowers all around her and to once again admire the impeccable landscape. As JoVonna drove the short distance to Raphael's dress shop, she listened to the radio and wondered what the mayor must be thinking after their last conversation. Turning to the task at hand, JoVonna walked up to the door of the shop. Raphael greeted her with a glass of champagne and beckoned for her to have a seat while he unveiled what was in his words, a masterpiece. The black, floor-length dress fit perfectly, and when Raphael added the wide, sequined belt, JoVonna was pleased. She agreed with the accessories Raphael had chosen and handed him a check. As she was leaving, Raphael wished her good luck with the speech she was making, and JoVonna glanced at her watch and hurried out of the shop so as not to be late for her facial and pedicure in preparation for the next evening.

THE RAIN WILL TELL
Chapter Seven

Mayor Marcus Brackner sat quietly as the Councilmen all tabled topics of concern regarding Richland Hills. After the last item on the agenda had been resolved or placed on the calendar for more discussion at a later date, the mayor stood slowly. He was visibly angry as he began to speak.

"All of you here are very familiar with JoVonna Rossier. She is the most influential woman in this community and she definitely has the most money, which generally buys her whatever she wants. Ms. Rossier has made it perfectly clear that she is not pleased with the position that I have taken towards her neighbors living on that land. She contends that the land they live on is rightfully still hers, and she has informed me that she has the power to persuade the vast majority of my constituents to vote me out of office in the next election. I believe that if she sets her mind to it, she can convince a lot of people in this town to vote for whomever she chooses. After all, most of these folks know that she could buy some serious trouble for them at the drop of a hat and no one wants that. In conclusion, gentlemen, I am asking for your undivided support. I want current reports on my position in the community. Let me know what you are hearing. I intend to advertise more. I've got an upcoming spot on the radio and Lilly is having her printing company make some posters and samples for billboards. I want you all to interact with the people in your districts. I know that as employees of the city, you cannot publicly endorse me, but I want you to find out what kind of door-to-door and telephone responses we are getting. Hell, I have worked my butt off to serve this community. I have been involved in everything from upgrading the standard of living for the elderly to trying to entice new business to this town so that the younger generations coming up will have a choice as to whether or not they want their employer to be Ms. Rossier. I'm not going to lose it all to some megabitch who happens to be unhappy with her neighbors. Hell, I know some folks in this town still talk out loud about the fact that they believe JoVonna's daddy's bad business deal is the reason Virgil gave those people that land. I can't help that! I have a strong feeling that JoVonna is going to drop a bombshell at the Annual Mayor's Banquet. Otherwise, she would have canceled it after our last conversation, even if it did mean forfeiting the money she spent and the opportunity to be the keynote speaker."

Mayor Brackner stood there silently, his eyes asking for assistance. He had to meet a deadline on some paperwork, so he turned and left the conference room, leaving the others sitting there. A quick glance around the room made it painfully obvious that there were some very strong opinions about the subject the mayor had just opened.

Councilman Adolphus Fleming took a long and very noisy drink from the coffee cup that sat in front of him. When he finished, he cleared his throat and posed a question to all those present. "Just what exactly does Ms. Rossier want this time?"

Councilman Wilbert Smith stood up to redistribute his weight and tucked a fresh chew of tobacco into his jaw. "Aw hell, ya'll all know the story well as I do. JoVonna's daddy and the former mayor had a real nasty fallin' out. JoVonna believes her family got their name smeared when Virgil left that land to them families from Greenspoint. Folks felt like JoVonna's daddy should have found a way to make him sell it back or give it back, but not turn it over to them families. I reckon the town's folk did have a lot of meetings after they knowed them people was moving to Richland Hills. Somebody even burned a few crosses, but them families, they just sung a lot of songs, read them Bibles and did what that highfalutin' lawyer of theirs said for them to do. It wasn't until a while back that they could even trade in this town. Every Saturday, them women folk of theirs would get up at the crack of dawn and catch the bus to Greenspoint to get groceries. They carried them Bibles with them everywhere they went. Then come a time when one of them saved that little Turner girl's life. She was 'bout to be electrocuted from a downed live wire after one of them bad rains. He lost one of his arms helpin' her, and her moma start lettin' them trade at her store at night, after the white folks' business hours was done. They paid their bills on time, and gradually other folks started lettin' them trade in their stores too. One of 'em even went to see old Doc Busby when he cracked his head open tryin' to put a roof on that old makeshift church they built. Doc Busby said they paid him in full, and that night they left a mess of the best fried chicken he ever tasted along with two pound cakes on his doorstep. He won't let on, but I believe he birthed that set of colored twins, too. Anyhow, JoVonna, she ain't give up on wantin' to get them off of that land that Virgil refused to sell back to her daddy. She still got fifteen-- twenty acres of land to the North, but them houses is situated just about an acre downhill from her on the South.

The thing is, the land is rightfully theirs, whether some of the folk in this town like it or not. Hell, Virgil even left enough money in that account of theirs for taxes to be paid on them houses and the land for the next ten years or so, and they been right timely 'bout following up on their tax notices. Once that lawyer let them know they was allowed to, they started comin' in the office to see that they was given proper credit for paying their taxes every year. The tax assessor just subtracts from the balance the amount due for their taxes each year. Ya'll know, I believe they went and got themselves a copy of Virgil's Will and they hired that boy who I hear tell got educated up north. He come in with them to the readin' of the Will. After the readin' was done, they all went over there and spread out pallets on the land their houses was gonna be built on, and he made everything real plain for them. Folks got real mad when that lawyer of theirs hired them construction boys from over in Greenspoint to come in here and build them houses. Word is, he taught them how to keep real good track of that money. Hell, I believe each one of them families got some way of keepin' track of how much is left in their account. If that ain't enough, I heard that damned suit-wearing lawyer of theirs even showed them how to calculate the interest due on their money." The Councilman spat into a cup. "Ain't really much we can do, even if some of us had a mind to. Ya'll know that the most they do is sit on their porches readin' to them nappy-headed offspring of theirs and keep the smell of fried chicken in the air. On Sundays they gather in that little clapboard church they built on that piece of land that sticks out behind their houses. A couple of fellas over at the shop said we should have burned them houses down the day they finished building them, but they had enough money to rebuild them houses two times over. A lot of things come to mind in the way of getting rid of 'em and satisfying Ms. JoVonna, but I don't want their blood on my hands. Besides, that lawyer would just have a whole army of them Northerners in them fancy cars down here turning Richland Hills inside out. I don't want nothing to do with it, and if the rest of you is smart, you'll leave them alone, at least until we get somethin' else to mess with 'em 'bout. We already know that ain't none of the rest of they kinfolks over in Greenspoint, or anywhere else in Mississippi got the money to move in here. They will probably die off sooner or later from some of them diseases of theirs, and Richland Hills will go back to the way it used to be. Now, how we gonna make sure Marcus wins this next election despite what Ms. Rossier is aimin' to do?"

Marcus Brackner sat in his recently painted office, which contained only a wooden desk, two chairs, a large round table and two bookshelves. The mayor was mildly curious about why the meeting he left in the conference room more than an hour ago was still in session. He smiled to himself and tried to envision those in attendance trying to turn their staunch support for him into their own campaign slogans. Marcus finished some paperwork on his desk while he waited for a telephone call from Miss Lilly Parker, the woman who had been his constant companion for almost three years now. He planned to propose to her soon. Lilly was plain and pretty at the same time. She was tall and slender, with unruly short black hair and intense green eyes. She wore virtually no cosmetics, and her eyes and the tiny dimple on the left side of her smile were her most attractive facial features. Marcus loved the way her skin felt. He had committed her fragrance to memory. She was strong and intelligent and taught Marcus what it was like to have a woman love him totally. For a moment, Marcus reflected back on the evening he had gone to JoVonna's mansion for the party she had given in his honor. JoVonna had offered her body to him as a reward for ridding her of the neighbors she despised, and Marcus knew now that even if he had come up with a plan right then and there, he would have regretted it if he had slept with JoVonna. She was by far one of the most beautiful women in Richland Hills and Marcus wondered how someone as pretty as she was on the outside could be so ugly on the inside.

The intercom interrupted Marcus' thoughts.

"Mayor Brackner?"

"Yes."

"Miss Lilly Parker is on line one."

"Thanks. Send the call through."

"Good afternoon, Lilly."

"Hello Marcus. I've just come from Rothchilds. I was in there picking up my dress and shoes for the banquet and I'll tell you, the southern tongues are wagging. The general consensus is that Miss Rossier is powerfully upset with you over some issue that you have failed to remedy for her, and she intends to show you just who wears the biggest pants in this town."

"Now honey, don't you worry. You go on out and get your hair done for that banquet tomorrow. I'll pick up my tuxedo as soon as I can get out of here. I am still waiting for the council members to adjourn. Don't you concern yourself with this at all. I'm sure that no matter what Miss Rossier may have in store for me, that my loyal supporters will somehow see to it that I am re-elected." Marcus put the receiver back in its cradle and glanced at his watch, noting that the eight people he left in a meeting over an hour ago were still in the conference room with the door closed.

Marcus picked up his briefcase and hat and informed his secretary that he was out for the day. He hesitated momentarily in front of the elevators, debating whether he should go back into the meeting to see what new campaign strategies they had come up with, but then decided against it. He was feeling surer of his re-election now; he knew the council was working diligently for him. After all, he had a tuxedo to pick up and shoes to be shined. He had to get his hair trimmed and buy a corsage for Miss Lilly. Marcus cursed himself for being such a procrastinator and got on the elevator. When the doors to that conference room finally did open, eight straight-faced people emerged, ready to focus on the campaign and to do whatever it would take to get Marcus re-elected.

Chapter Eight

The residents of Richland Hills woke up to a warm and sunny day, and JoVonna was delighted as she was gently tugged from a light sleep by the smell of honeysuckle growing in abundance just outside her bedroom window. She waited impatiently, drawn to the aroma of the fresh coffee Margot was preparing. JoVonna's thoughts ventured back into the past–nearly a year ago–to the secret plans that she and Margot had made in the guest room, right next to her bedroom.

They buried a boy that night and the result was a heinous bargaining tool that JoVonna now had against Margot. Almost a year ago, she returned home early from a speaking engagement to find Margot's face swollen and streaked with tears. In between sobs, Margot managed to tell JoVonna what happened. She invited her lover over for dinner and they had become sexually aroused. Margot took him to one of the guest bedroom suites because they were decorated much more expensively than her quarters. Margot was completely naked when she noticed some movement outside the window and whispered to her lover that she felt like someone was watching them. He told her to put on her robe and walk back and forth in front of the window to create a distraction. He said that he would sneak through the gardens and check it out. A few minutes later, Margot heard what sounded like an animal in pain, and then a snapping, cracking noise that seemed to echo into the night.

When Margot's companion returned, he was wet with perspiration. He wrung his hands together as he told her that there had been a colored boy about twelve years old peering into the window. He said he believed that he had broken the boy's neck. He left him lying just outside the window. Margot's companion got dressed, took some money out of her purse, and said he was leaving. Margot was still very scared and upset as she finished telling JoVonna what happened earlier in the evening. The thought of someone lying dead just outside the window chilled her. She pulled the curtain back again and those wide-open eyes that seemed to be staring at her out of that dead black face made her scream. JoVonna shook her until she stopped. JoVonna made a drink for herself and made Margot have one as well. She instructed Margot to get dressed, telling her that they were going to bury the boy. Margot protested and wanted to call the police. She became hysterical and JoVonna slapped her across the face with the back of her hand. Margot got up off the floor, and together they went out into the rain and buried the boy in between two trees. The pouring rain that evening hid the footprints and by morning, all evidence was completely washed away.

The newspapers discounted the boy's disappearance as a runaway and Margot knew from that day on that she would always be at JoVonna's mercy. JoVonna knew it as well, and even though they never spoke of what happened that night again, the incident left a presence in the mansion as thick as an early-morning London fog. JoVonna took some deep breaths to shake off her thoughts of the past and clear the liquor clouds in her head. She climbed out of bed.

"Margot, bring me some coffee, and get my hairdresser on the telephone. Draw a bath for me and bring in the newspaper. Today is my big day, and I want to look as beautiful as I feel." JoVonna continued to bark out instructions as she took her coffee into her library for her morning ritual of watching the people at the bottom of the hill and making more notes on possible ways to get rid of them by any means possible. Several minutes later, JoVonna walked back to the liquor cabinets in the kitchen to add some gin to her coffee and found Margot on her hands and knees scrubbing up the mess that JoVonna made the night before in a drunken stupor. JoVonna leaned across the counter and almost laughed aloud at the sight of someone like Margot on all fours scrubbing the floors.

"Margot, you know that I will be out this evening, and I may chose to stay and socialize for a while after the Mayor's banquet. I overheard your telephone conversation, so I know that you have made plans with a man this evening."

Margot rolled her eyes upwards and cursed under her breath.

"I am sure that I don't have to remind you that you are never to have a man in my home again, so if you go out, stay out until your hormones have been neutralized. You can begin laying out my things as soon as you are finished there, and be a dear and go over to Raphael's and pick up the jewelry he selected for me. When you make out the butcher's list for this week, include fresh salmon. I am going to my library until time for my appointment."

Margot picked up the keys to the Cadillac she used for errands and thought to herself how different her life might have been had she not come to this town. She was broke and alone after her parents died and a brief modeling career she thought would support her education had failed her. She answered an ad in the Richland Hills Daily News that read:

WANTED: Young, single female to handle personal correspondence and some special projects. Private suite, car, clothing allowance, medical benefits, exposure to Richland Hill's upper crust. Salary negotiable.

Margot jumped at the opportunity and had since come to know a great deal about JoVonna. Still, she had mixed feelings about the lonely, obsessed, alcoholic, patronizing woman she worked for. Margot's thoughts were disrupted as she turned into the driveway of Raphael's shop. She was greeted by the short, fat and balding little man who challenged all whispered rumors that he had a preference for men with the excuse that he was waiting for a modern-day Mona Lisa to share his riches and his future. Everywhere

30

Margot went that day, she found Richland Hills residents getting facials and manicures and taking extra measures to make themselves beautiful; some of them maximized their credit limits for the event of the year - The Annual Mayor's Banquet.

JoVonna had just returned from her beauty appointment, where she had instructed her hairdresser to brush her hair back and hold it in place with combs with genuine diamond studs that Raphael had–with JoVonna's approval–sent over to the Cutting Edge Salon. When Margot walked through the doors from the gardens, JoVonna was pacing the floor, waiting for her.

"Margot, put those things away and make a drink for me. A double, and get me something for my headache. I left a list of things I want ready and waiting for me as soon as I am finished with my bath. Hurry Up! The later I am, the longer that pathetic excuse of a man you give yourself to will have to wait to relieve himself and leave you, the tramp that you are, sprawled out on worn out cotton sheets in a cheap hotel somewhere on the outskirts of town."

This was another one of the many times Margot pondered what it would be like to walk on JoVonna's face with spike heels. She knew that if JoVonna ever suspected that she wanted to leave the mansion forever that JoVonna would be on the telephone to the police before she could get out of the door. Margot did not want to go to jail, and she knew without a doubt that JoVonna would find a way to clear herself of having anything to do with that little boy buried in the yard and let her rot in jail. Margot went into the kitchen and begin to make out the list for the butcher. She snatched the list of household errands off the counter and began to gather all the things JoVonna had requested. When she finished, she made a fresh martini and sat it on a small table that stood just outside JoVonna's dressing room. Margot glanced at her watch and hurried to her suite at the back of the mansion to prepare for her own evening.

JoVonna hummed a soft and meaningless tune as she carefully stepped into the dress Raphael had tailored to her figure. She opened the door to allow some of the steam to evaporate. She was careful not to disturb her hair. JoVonna felt a smile cross her lips as she thought to herself what was about to transpire in just a matter of hours. She stepped into her black and silver evening slippers and, after carefully checking her makeup one last time in the mirror, walked to the rear of the mansion and opened the door to Margot's bedroom. Margot was startled and irritated by the fact that JoVonna entered her quarters any time she chose without knocking.

"I am going to be leaving in just a moment." JoVonna snapped. "Don't you forget what I told you."

Margot tilted and shook her head from side to side in silent mockery of JoVonna's admonishment and continued slipping the dress JoVonna had given her over her head. As JoVonna walked out through the gardens and down the path that led to her cars, the fragrance of honeysuckle was abundant in the evening air. She walked towards her Mercedes that stood gleaming under the floodlight of her garage. As JoVonna drove along, she laughed out loud as her thoughts centered on the plans she had for the incumbent mayor this evening. As she drew nearer to the ballroom where the Mayor's Banquet was to be hosted, she casually glanced out of the window, taking note of the groups of people arriving, collectively known as the "Who's Who" of Richland Hills. JoVonna recognized Glen Boyd and his wife along with some of the other council members. "Glen likes to write so much." she said aloud. "Well, I'll give him something to write about tonight! Then, maybe he can buy his wife something other than that appalling yellow dress she wears to every occasion." Several of the other people attending this event worked for her, either directly or indirectly. Others that were at the banquet openly supported her cause and she could probably bribe several of those who didn't. Those facts empowered her, giving her the courage to surge ahead with her plan. She allowed the valet to take temporary possession of her Mercedes and strode up the stairs that led into the brightly-lit ballroom. JoVonna walked slowly through the crowd, acknowledging those she chose to, ignoring the rest.

The orchestra set the tempo and several couples had already begun to dance. JoVonna took note of the long tables laden with duck and wild rice, hens with pecan stuffing, prime rib carved to order, Yorkshire pudding, a vegetable medley and a variety of other foods to satisfy any palate. There was also a table just for desserts with everything from pineapple upside down cake specially prepared in an iron skillet to fresh southern fruits sitting high atop a torte cake. The chefs wore starched white uniforms and stood at attention, ready to serve each dish. She was satisfied with the lovely flower arrangements as well as the china and crystal selections and over all, was well pleased with how her money had been spent to cater this affair.

JoVonna walked slowly, stopping to let the spotlight catch her dress as she headed towards her seat located right next to the podium. She smiled to camouflage laughter and nodded at the Mayor and Lilly Parker. After everyone was served, the master of ceremony stepped to the podium and enlightened the crowd with a few remarks about Mayor Marcus Brackner and then turned the evening over to the keynote speaker: JoVonna Rossier. JoVonna quickly swallowed the last of her third martini and took the podium.

"Ladies and Gentlemen, as you are well aware, each year I host a dinner party to honor the mayor and recognize his fine contributions to the City of Richland Hills and to his constituents. However; this year, I am afraid that I must inform you of some matters I feel that you as tax-paying residents of this community have a right to know....."

A hush fell over the crowd as JoVonna continued her speech. She took note of the attentive audience and paused a moment for emphasis.

"....You all know that several weeks ago, I hosted a party at my home in honor of this man who sits here and professes to be a fair-minded mayor for all of us. After the rest of the guests had gone for the evening, I asked the mayor to stay so that I might discuss with him the problem that is distressing all of us and causing a blemish on our community. I began to try to discuss with the mayor some ideas I had about ridding this community once and for all of those unwelcome people that have been thrust into our community. I suggested that we buy them out, and erect a monument on that land in memory of our families who founded this community. I quoted to him from the Richland Hills City Charter which clearly states that he has the power and the responsibility to define, prohibit, abate, suppress and prevent all things detrimental to the health, comfort, safety, convenience and welfare of the inhabitants of this city. The charter also states that the City has the power to obtain land and property. "

JoVonna held up a stack of papers and said, "I have the City Charter right here. I pleaded with the mayor, telling him that community will grow, and sooner or later they will want jobs in this town that you all should have. He laughed in my face and told me that it was true what folks say about how colored women can keep a bed cozier that a feathered comforter. He also told me that those women serve a good purpose in this community because they give him what he wants and do not pressure him for anything in return. He said that while Lilly was out of town--"

"You lying aristocratic bitch!" Lilly Parker screamed at JoVonna as she tripped over the mayor's chair trying to get to her. The mayor sat perfectly still. He was stunned and seemed to be unaware that Lilly had reached the podium and was clawing at JoVonna, ripping her dress off right there in front of everyone. Two of the waiters rushed forward and tried to pry Lilly's hands out of JoVonna's hair and salvage what remained of her dress, while wrapping her exposed breasts in a tablecloth. As JoVonna was helped off the stage, she turned to those present and yelled, "I am going to run for mayor. Your lives and this community will continue to suffer at the hands of this man." Lilly stood there fuming, holding a piece of the front of JoVonna's dress in her hands. Lilly and Marcus argued loudly, and she threatened to take a taxi home. "No. I will go get the car and take you home." Marcus said. The entire crowd was in an uproar. Some began arguing the points that JoVonna had made. Others, not wanting to make their opinions known publicly, just stared at what was going on around them.

One lone man stood quietly in the back of the ballroom. After a moment, he straightened his tie, looked around until he thought no one was watching, and casually left the ballroom. It was time for some things to change. He had prepared carefully, and now he was going to make the phone call that would set those changes in motion.

THE RAIN WILL TELL
Chapter Nine

JoVonna began to feel the full impact of the alcohol she had consumed much too quickly. She insisted on driving her Mercedes home, refusing to admit that she had too much to drink. She laughed out loud at the thought of what she had just done. She was too intoxicated to inventory the damage that Lilly had done to her gown and her hair. She stumbled up the hill and opened the door and yelled out Margot's name and then had to remind herself that Margot was out for the evening. JoVonna prepared another drink and threw a nightgown on her bed on her way to the shower. The mixture of the hot water and the excessive alcohol forced JoVonna to make her shower brief. After she slipped into her nightgown, she sat down in front of her mirror to brush her hair, and laughed aloud at her appearance. She threw the brush in the air and walked into the living room to make one last drink for herself before she retired for the evening. JoVonna tapped the side of the glass and fished out the olive with a long red fingernail and fell backwards onto the couch.

As she lay sleeping on the couch, there were two men outside the mansion who had arrived in Mississippi just over an hour earlier. They sat on top of the eight-foot wall that almost surrounded the back of JoVonna's mansion. The two men had received explicit instructions via an anonymous call from someone in Richland Hills. The task at hand seemed mundane to them. They were professionals in their field. The exceptions to the norm in this case were that they never came face to face with their employer and they were paid in advance. They had to go to the outskirts of town, but found all of their money, just as the muffled voice had promised, under the floorboard in an old bank. Without speaking, the two men worked together as though they were receiving their instructions from a shared brain. The taller of the two men threw a piece of plywood down onto the ground. His hands had been submerged in a mixture of candle wax and a very thin plastic substance that would not readily be observed by an untrained eye, even in daylight, but would leave no fingerprints. He jumped down onto the plywood with the quickness and agility of a cat while the second man lowered down several more pieces of plywood, which the first man formed into a single line that led directly through the gardens and to the back entrance of the mansion. Each time he laid a piece of wood just in front of the other, he returned for another piece until quickly and quietly, he had completed laying a plywood path from the wall to the back door. When this was complete, the second man emerged from the wall just as quickly as the first. Dressed in business suits, they walked towards the door, oblivious to the rain that had started to fall. The men opened the door with ease and entered the mansion through the kitchen. Each one carried a briefcase and a gun in his waistband. They split up and moved ahead cautiously, making sure no one else was in the house.

Just as she was entering the second stage of sleep, JoVonna, believing she heard a sound, opened one lazy eye. She rose up, thinking she must be dreaming, as she gazed through hazy eyes at the two men walking towards her. JoVonna used all of her strength to raise her drunken and uncoordinated body to a sitting position and asked in a voice that she tried to make sound authoritative and unafraid, "What the hell are you doing in my home?"

The two men took seats and began to explain to her that they had been informed of the problem she was having gaining control of the property that her neighbors owned, and that they were there to help her.

"You see, madam, we were made aware of your problems through someone who wants to help you, but at the same time, chooses to remain anonymous. That is the reason for all of the secrecy, and that is the reason we had to come in this way." JoVonna pondered who would have sent these men and figured it must have been Marcus. He must have come to his senses. She laughed to herself.

While the first man continued with his story, the second man opened his briefcase that contained several copies of Deeds of Trust and Title Company documents that had been stolen, forged and left at the abandoned bank for them to further convince JoVonna of what they wanted her to believe.

"We have a contract here that one of the families has signed. They are willing to sell their property to you, if you will agree to pay each of the other families the same amount."

JoVonna interrupted and slurred. "I offered to pay each of them $10,000 for their land some time ago and they refused. They just stood there singing some religious song and then turned their backs on me."

"Well, they are asking just a bit more than the amount you offered them, but with a little gentle persuasion from us, they will sell you all of that land. They want fifteen thousand each in cash. All you have to do is trust us.

What we need for you to do is show us what information you have about them that you think could be useful and we will take that information and use it to make sure they don't change their minds about selling their property to you."

JoVonna's half-opened eyes scanned the contract the man placed in front of her and tried to focus on its contents.

"Okay." She slurred. I will give each of the families $15,000 to move out, but how much is it going to cost for you to conduct this business for me?" JoVonna asked.

Both men looked at each other, and again, as if their minds were synchronized, immediately realized the opportunity for a bonus. They would have the money that had been left at the bank for them as well as JoVonna's unexpected offer to give them more than the $15,000 per household they had been instructed to ask for. The older of the two men leaned forward, and explained to JoVonna that the opportunity to free herself from her unwanted neighbors would cost her only $20,000 for their assistance. He also explained again that the money would have to be paid in cash, so that no one would ever know about this transaction. He said that with no paper trail, it would be easier to convince everyone that those families chose to sell and leave of their own will. Seeing that the combination of JoVonna's drunken stupor, their business suits and the counterfeit documents had convinced her, the two men asked JoVonna to join them in a celebration drink. JoVonna stood, with some effort, and walked over to the bar to begin pouring the drinks. All the time, she continued to talk about all of the evidence she had gathered about her neighbors and how they were a disgrace to the community. While she was on her feet, one of the men suggested that she go and get the evidence, and asked if she had all of the cash available. She replied yes and started to leave the room, with one of the men following her. She stopped him and asked, "Why didn't you gentlemen just come to the front door?"

"We had to make sure you would listen to our plan, and we knew that we could explain it much better this way, rather than trying to explain our plans through a closed door in the middle of the night. Besides, if this little deal gets dirty and we have to use force to get your neighbors out, people may speculate, but we guarantee there won't be any evidence pointing directly back to you. That is what you want, isn't it?"

JoVonna agreed and continued to explain about all of the pictures she had taken of the families and other things she thought were unfitting for this community. She closed the door to her study and stood counting stacks of money from her safe. The second man laughed as he pulled a vile from his briefcase and emptied the contents into JoVonna's glass. A few minutes later, when JoVonna returned from her study, she took a seat across from the two men and laid the bundles of money on the table.

"Gentlemen, this is money well spent. Who arranged for you to come here tonight? It had to be someone at the banquet. Was it Marcus?"

Instead of offering an answer, both men picked up their drinks, and encouraged JoVonna to do likewise. "Here is to changes." Glasses clinked. JoVonna finished her drink in two long gulps, and stuck her finger in the glass to retrieve the olive as the two men sat and watched. A few minutes later when she slumped over on the couch, the men went to work, gathering all three glasses, pouring the contents in the toilet and putting the glasses in a plastic bag in one of the briefcases where the money had been placed. They took back all of the documents they brought, as well as the documents, money and pictures that JoVonna had produced. As they lifted her off of the couch, the younger of the two men commented on how beautiful she was and kissed her and fondled her breasts to make sure that she was completely under the influence of the drug.

When they reached the bedroom, and placed her in her bed to make it appear as though she was sleeping, the older of the two men went to make sure they had removed everything. Then he went to the bar and poured half a martini with an olive and took it back to her bedroom to set it beside her bed. The younger man had partially undressed and penetrated JoVonna when his partner walked into the room.

"What the hell are you doing?"

"What difference does it make? She will never know. Even if she were to regain consciousness, she has so much alcohol and narticystozil in her system that she would probably have a hard time remembering her own name."

"Yeah, well, if she ever remembers you had sex with her, she will probably personally dig a hole, put you in it, and have a prison built on top of you."

The younger man laughed. After he dressed, he straightened her nightgown and repositioned her on the bed.

Both men backtracked to make sure they had not missed any evidence. They left the same way they came, picking up the boards one by one until they reached the wall and threw the boards and briefcases over. The two men scaled the wall with ease and drove the van back to the rear of the bank. Their employer sat in a plain black car in the shadows watching them. Once inside, they changed into dry clothes and raincoats, placing plastic bags that contained their shares of the money inside of the raincoats. They poured gasoline on the van, the briefcases, the boards, the rubber boots and everything else inside and set it on fire. They ran about half a block where they found a rental car that had been rented locally and left for them. Inside, they found two plane tickets with different destinations. Each man addressed a package to himself and placed his share of the money inside.

While their employer watched from the shadows of two adjoining buildings, they put the money that JoVonna had given them to buy the families' homes in a laundry bag they had been told would be in the back seat of the car. They drove to the airport. Each man placed his package in a mail drop just outside the airport entrance. They looked at one another, silently declaring a job well done, and headed towards separate terminals. Neither man had to ask about the destination of the other. What they already knew was that one would head east, the other west, and that slowly they would work their way back to the Midwest. The car had been left in a parking lot near the back, just as the two men had been instructed. Shortly after they entered the airport, their employer put his gun back in his waistband. He walked quickly out of the darkness to the rental car. He counted the money and drove into Richland Hills. He paid cash for the rental the next morning and walked out of the rental agency with the credit card and imprint in his hand. He threw the stolen credit card that he had used to rent the car down a sewer drain. He lit a cigarette and stuck the hot ember to the edge of the credit card slip and let it burn and then dropped it into a barrel that contained a glowing fire vacated by

41

vagrants. The rain produced a hissing noise as it fell slightly, but proved to be no opponent for the roaring fire. He took a taxi to the airport to get his own car. He pulled over on the way back to Richland Hills and threw away a small bag that contained a hairpiece and eyeglasses.

THE RAIN WILL TELL
Chapter Ten

Margot opened the back door and looked at the clock on the kitchen wall. It was 7:00 a.m. She had intended to be home by 5:00. She swore softly and went into the living room where the stench of liquor was almost overbearing. Believing that everything was in order, she went to her room and undressed quickly. Hazy from last evening's activities, Margot put together a mental breakfast for JoVonna and collapsed across her bed.

Late into the morning, a red-eyed Margot arose and stood in the shower, feeling the effects of the steaming hot water pricking her skin like tiny little needles, reviving her tired body and at the same time, clearing her head for the argument she was sure she was going to have with JoVonna. If the information that Margot was hearing on the news about The Mayor's Banquet last evening were true, then JoVonna would be on the warpath today, and she would take no prisoners. Margot slipped into her clothes and went up to the front of the mansion. She went to the refrigerator for eggs, fruit and sausage. She rounded the corner to the dining room and was surprised to find that JoVonna had not yet come out of her bedroom. Normally, the more JoVonna drank the night before, the earlier she got up to raise hell the next day. Margot started the coffee while she took out fresh croissants and both of JoVonna's favorite jams. She decided to take JoVonna a cup of coffee and a croissant before she began to slice the fruit. As Margot approached JoVonna, she realized that she was sleeping more soundly than was normal, even for an alcoholic. Margot tried several times to awaken JoVonna, and when she got no response, she decided that she would put JoVonna in a nice hot tub to bring her around. While Margot was drawing the bath, the stray cat she had been feeding slipped in through the open window and upset the breakfast tray while trying to get the thick cream. The

43

cat was frightened by the breaking dishes and retreated out of the window.

When Margot returned and saw that the tray was in disarray, she assumed that JoVonna had stirred long enough to try to eat breakfast and passed out again. This minimized the thought that Margot had that maybe something was wrong. She put her hands on her hips and looked down at JoVonna lying on the bed.

"Wake up, JoVonna. Your breakfast is almost ready. Don't you want to finish your coffee?"

She looked at the overturned coffee cup and breathed out a sigh through hair that was now hanging down in her face. Frustrated, she threw an oversized pillow onto the floor, rolled JoVonna off the bed and onto the pillow, and pulled the edge of the pillow, which eliminated the task of trying to physically carry JoVonna to the bathroom.

She put JoVonna's legs in the tub first and then lifted her from behind like a wheelbarrow into the tub. JoVonna's head slumped and she showed no signs of waking up. As a final effort, Margot turned on more hot water and poured in plenty of the perfumed soaps that JoVonna loved, hoping that either the hot water or the aroma would bring JoVonna around. As Margot turned to reach for a sponge, JoVonna's head fell backwards, hitting the tub with a sickening thud. Margot saw the blood and panicked. She threw the sponge down and pulled the top half of her body out of the tub. She removed the plug so that JoVonna would not fall back into the water and drown. Next, she ran to the telephone to call for an ambulance. She snatched a robe from the trunk at the foot of JoVonna's bed, ran back to the bathroom and wrestled the other half of JoVonna's body out of the tub and onto the floor. Margot was wet with water from the tub and her own perspiration from trying to get the robe on JoVonna. As much as she disliked her, she could not let an obviously drunken woman who was still to some, a pillar of the community be subjected to perfect strangers coming into her home and seeing her completely naked. When the

44

ambulance attendants arrived, they immediately bandaged JoVonna's head, took her blood pressure, checked her heart rate and started to bombard Margot with questions at such a rate that she became flustered. As they were taking JoVonna to the ambulance, one of the attendants called ahead to the hospital. Margot ran back to the mansion, turned off the food, grabbed her keys and followed the ambulance to the hospital.

While she was sitting in the emergency room, Margot was temporarily distracted as she noticed one of the reporters who covered all of the newsworthy stories in the small community of Richland Hills in the corridor. He was covering the story of a young white girl who had been beaten. The camera captured the fear on her swollen, bruised face. The lower half of the hospital gown she had changed into concealed the worst of her injuries. From her bed, she talked into the camera, describing the black boy with hands as strong as iron that just kept hitting and touching her. A fifteen-year- old black boy lay in a hospital bed across town, near death. The girl's father had grabbed him and beat him when he was found walking on a street near their house. The boy stuttered, which meant his answers about why he was in that neighborhood did not come fast enough for the girl's father who questioned and beat him at the same time. When the police got to the hospital, the young boy swore that he had never even seen the young white girl in the picture they showed him. He had certainly not touched her. The girl feared her father and the warning to keep silent that she read in his eyes far too much to ever tell the camera crew, or even her mother what had really happened in basement of their home. Seeing her father's clenched fist as he spoke on her behalf was enough to send the truth to a place in her memory where no one would ever know it. She pulled her covers up closer around her chin and signaled for the camera to be turned off. The reporter turned just in time to see JoVonna Rossier lying in the room across from the girl with a nurse working frantically over her. He ran up to the emergency

45

room attendants and then the doctor, demanding to know the nature of JoVonna's illness. Soon, all attention was focused on JoVonna, who lay motionless on the bed, her skin colorless. Doctors responded to the code of STAT and rushed past the inquiring reporter to the room that JoVonna had been taken to for examination. The hospital staff blocked the reporter's camera and JoVonna's condition was not disclosed to the reporter- not one word. Margot rested on one foot and then the other as she stood at the nurses' station, frustrated and irritated with the questions the nurses were asking her in order to complete JoVonna's chart. Practically everyone already knew who JoVonna was, and word of her condition, which would vary according to who was telling the story, would most certainly spread throughout this town. There would be the reporter's version and there would be the southern women's version.

Margot took a seat and waited, her mind flashing back to the mansion. She tried to get a mental picture of everything she had seen as she rushed around the mansion that morning. She talked to herself now. "Let's see, there was JoVonna lying there in the bed, with that drink next to her, which was not unusual for her." At first thought, Margot could only surmise that JoVonna had exceeded even her own alcoholic limit this time. She sat back as she reassured herself that one of the doctors would come into the room any minute and inform her that JoVonna would be back to being the bitch that she was in no time at all. Margot put her hand to her mouth as if it would stifle her thought. She watched the hours pass as the white uniforms of the nurses on duty soon became no more than a blur. Margot's eyes began to feel as though someone had attached weights to them. She put her purse underneath her head and dozed off into what she thought was a bad dream; however, when she opened her eyes, the dream would not go away. The doctors were standing there, calling her name and looking down at her, somber faced. They informed her in medical terms, and then again in layman's terms that JoVonna had lapsed into a coma and that further tests would be necessary. The doctors stood on either side of Margot. One of them handed her a cup of coffee, the other explained to her that JoVonna's situation was rare, not something that either of them had ever seen before, and that they may even have to confer with other doctors who may have seen patients with JoVonna's symptoms for a diagnosis. Margot felt her head start to whirl as the reality of the situation set in. JoVonna was comatose and none of the doctors knew how she came to be this way or even if she would ever come out of the coma. Margot drank two cups of coffee, one right after the other and then slowly began to make a mental list of the things that must be done. She would have to assume responsibility for all matters at the mansion which meant that she would have to speak with JoVonna's attorneys about ensuring that expenses associated with the mansion were maintained for however long JoVonna remained comatose. She got out a piece of paper and started to write. She would also have to call Shirley at Rossier Industries and inform the Board Members and officers of JoVonna's various businesses, and since JoVonna had no immediate family, the next matter of importance as Margot saw it was to address JoVonna's personal calendar. She anticipated that there would be a lot of phone calls, both from those that would express sincere concern, and those who simply wanted to know what was going on in this powerful woman's life.

Margot shook her head to try to slow down the thoughts that were now flooding into her mind. She took one more long look at the limp body of her employer that lay like a rag doll in the hospital bed. Subconsciously, Margot became aware of all of the machines and monitors that were being used to indicate JoVonna's condition. She decided to herself that collectively, this must be modern technology at its finest. Nothing was spared for the Grand Lady of Richland Hills. Margot decided that the first thing she must do was to get some sleep to clear her head. Once again she thought about the fact that, for a while, she would be responsible for running the mansion and that she would play a very important role in helping to keep JoVonna's business itinerary on track. A smile crossed her lips before she realized it.

THE RAIN WILL TELL
Chapter Eleven

Margot kept busy for the remainder of the weekend and awakened fresh and feeling invigorated early on that following Monday morning. The first thing that dawned on her was that she would be making coffee only for herself and cooking breakfast to suit her own needs this morning, and once again she found it hard to suppress a smile. Immediately after she had showered and prepared breakfast, she called JoVonna's office to set up a meeting with the attorneys and the Board of Directors. Having completed that, she reserved the rest of the morning for going over JoVonna's calendar and appointment book. She made a note of which of the attorneys had JoVonna's proxy and decided to speak with him after she jotted down a few notes. She had signature authority on a small household expense account and she wanted to have that increased. Margot wrote down a message that she would leave for Timothy Wells, the Vice President of Rossier Industries.

The phone began to ring and Margot looked at the clock and decided that not even God would be calling this early, and she surely did not intend to answer for anyone else, at least not until she decided what she would tell them. She munched a piece of toast as she prepared a statement for newspapers, the two major television stations in Richland Hills, and the stations in the surrounding areas that carried Richland Hills news. Margot looked down at the list she had prepared the night before. There were several people that needed to be notified of JoVonna's condition. She made more notes in an attempt to offset what the press might fabricate out of sheer speculation. No one had been informed of the true nature of JoVonna's ailment, mainly because the doctors were still not sure what caused her to continue to lie there comatose in her hospital bed.

Days turned into weeks and weeks into months as JoVonna continued to lie motionless in her hospital bed. In their continued and thorough examinations, the doctors discovered that JoVonna was pregnant. Since no one inquired about her pregnancy, the doctors assumed this was something she either had not known or that she knew and had chosen to keep to herself. Since neither doctor wanted to be sued for breech of patient confidentiality, they didn't tell anyone. They increased her intravenous feedings, working feverishly to provide nourishment for the unborn child.

Margot spoke with board members at Rossier Industries almost daily and provided them with the sketchy details of JoVonna's progress as she received them from the doctors. She also stayed in close contact with the attorneys. Margot applauded herself for having made remarkable progress in attending to JoVonna's affairs while she was comatose. Nearly all of the board members were reluctant to let Margot be privy to the intimate details of JoVonna's company, but she developed a much better sense of what the corporate world was about through Timothy Wells, JoVonna's vice president. He took the time to make sure she understood the different procedures associated with Rossier Industries. They had lunch in his office on several occasions. He taught her how business knowledge could make a person rich. She, in turn, used bedroom knowledge to get the business knowledge she needed.

Each time Margot called the hospital, the doctors still had not been able to diagnose what had caused JoVonna's coma; however, they had made several notes pertaining to her alcohol level the day she had been brought into the hospital four months ago. They were simply working now to try to save the unborn child and to provide JoVonna with adequate nourishment.

The following Tuesday was another day as usual for Margot, who stopped by the flower shop on the way up to JoVonna's room. She would go in and check on JoVonna, confer with the doctors and then get on with the business at hand for the day.

The whole town buzzed with the news that its most prominent citizen was still hospitalized. While the beauty shop circuit had one version of what must have been the fate of Ms. JoVonna Rossier, other businesses and places the townsfolk frequented each had their own rendition of what happened that night four months ago.

Many of the townsfolk feared that if the doctors could not find out what held JoVonna nearly lifeless in a coma, that her businesses would suffer and maybe even fall into more evil hands and pose an even greater threat than she did. Those that knew everything that had happened over the years found it truly amazing to actually realize that this one woman controlled the financial sustenance of so many of the residents of Richland Hills.

It was a humid and hazy day in Richland Hills and a trail of white sheets and beautiful handmade quilts hung on the makeshift clotheslines behind the modest homes in the community within a community where Bessie Smith and Willie Mae Gibson lived. They spoke quietly amongst themselves about the goings on in JoVonna's large mansion that appeared to deliberately stick its front out through a mass of mature oak trees and climbing honeysuckle vines. Bessie and Willie Mae sat rocking on Willie Mae's front porch, stopping only to refill their canning jars from a pitcher of cold lemonade. Willie Mae leaned forward, wiping her hands on the red and white patchwork apron that covered her ample physique.

"Miss Willie Mae."

"What you want now, gal?"

"What you 'spose done really happened to Miss JoVonna? It's been quite a spell since she come 'round here botherin' us now. She give me the shimmies wearin' them dead animals round huh neck an' all."

51

Willie Mae raised herself out of the wooden swing where she had been seated and walked over to light the hard bread that she burned in an old iron skillet to keep the Mississippi flies away. "That stench be awful, but taint no flies be lightin' on Willie Mae this day, naw suh."

Rubbing her shiny black face to recollect her thoughts, Willie Mae looked over at Bessie. "Gal, ain't nobody educated you?" It be fashionable for Miss JoVonna to wear them foxes an' such round huh neck. That one thing what show she got much money as she do. I hear tell she still layin' there in that hospital bed. All them good looks she had goin' sho' need re-doing if she ever come out of there. I hear at the grocery sto' she be lookin' like a ghost. She ain't movin'. Theys havin' to attend to huh needs jus' like a newborn baby. We be knowin' for sho' when Miss JoVonna come back to that there mansion. That side faces us will showly be lit up agin. And, I reckon that feelin' will come to me that I gets when she in that house. A feelin' like someone 'sides the Good Lawd be lookin' down on me."

Bessie straightened out her long calico skirt and turned to Willie Mae. "You 'spose when she do come home she be comin' round here in that big fancy car tellin' us to get out agin'?"

"I reckon she be botherin' us agin shortly, child. She be wantin' this land even if she don't never do nuthin with it. One time she come by here and say, if we was born in Greenspoint, then we ought to go home and die there. Mr. Russell, that law man from up north what been so kind and all, he say he still got things under control for us an' not to fuss over it none. Miss JoVonna, she be the devil's companion. Naw child, we ain't seen the last of huh, but don't you weary nun. Mr. Russell, that law man be comin' to see us agin soon."

THE RAIN WILL TELL
Chapter Twelve

Even though it had rained earlier that morning, causing problems for the motorist as well as the pedestrians in the town of Richland Hills, Marcus' supporters turned out in full force for the rally that was taking place just weeks prior to the polls opening to re-elect him as mayor. Many of the townsfolk still shuddered at the thought of what would have happened if JoVonna had been able to act on her announcement that she intended to be mayor of Richland Hills. Since JoVonna still lay comatose in the hospital and Marcus' only opponent was not worthy of winning the town's loyalty away from him, he was sure to be able to continue to carry out his plans to continue to improve Richland Hills for at least one more term.

With the sun peaking through and promising to warm the afternoon, the overall spirit of the crowd that gathered was light. Children danced to the tunes of the band and stopped frequently to play in the street. They ran to catch up to their mothers and fathers on the way to where the stage had been constructed for the mayor to speak. Everyone present, including the media knew that this story would have taken on a different twist if Ms. Rossier would have had her way. There were those that feared that if she came out of the coma any time soon, that she would start up right where she left off... raising hell.

Ms. Rossier had her followers, and they believed just as she did, that she should continue in her pursuit to drive those families out of town and regain ownership of that land, to undo what Virgil had done. Many of them were brazen enough to openly discuss their views and say they agreed with JoVonna that those families should go back to Greenspoint. Several others though, wore two hats, whichever of the two best suited their own needs at the time.

The local newspaper quoted Marcus Brackner as saying that he wanted the town of Richland Hills to be the same town for our children as it had been for us, peaceful, prosperous and beautiful. The mayor was careful to sidestep any reference to what happened at the Mayor's Ball, but Miss Lilly was a constant reminder to all those present as she sat perfectly still with her back as straight as an ironing board in a chair on the right-hand side of the stage. Marcus addressed an enthusiastic crowd, reminding them of his record and assuring them that he had solid plans for the future of Richland Hills. Once the rally was over, the people of Richland Hills went about their business as usual, and City Hall was no exception. With the mayor's re-election practically sewn up, the council members had their tasks before them. Since JoVonna was unable to interfere as she had so much in the past, they were able to get on with the issues that really affected Richland Hills.

Chapter Thirteen

Margot went about the business at hand at the mansion as though she were a programmed soldier, all the time learning more about what it took to keep it running smoothly and enjoying the time she had alone. Still, she visited the hospital every day, and as always, the doctor's reports were the same. JoVonna was still comatose. The only thing that was changing was the size of the baby growing inside of her. Since Margot was not directly related to JoVonna, the information about JoVonna's rapid surge into motherhood was still withheld, and it was decided that any questions that were asked about JoVonna's weight gain would be attributed to bloating and poor circulation.

JoVonna's condition was discussed frequently and discretely amongst the attending physicians and it was decided very early on that information about her impending pregnancy would be detailed in a separate medical chart. They each concurred that it would be better if they made certain that JoVonna was the one to disclose the information about her pregnancy to whomever she felt inclined to discuss it with. They had set up a consultation to divulge that particular information to Dr. Gregory Doyle, a physician in Detroit, Michigan who was known throughout the world for his reputation in treatment of comatose patients. Dr. Doyle would more than likely be consulted by telephone again, and possibly even asked to fly to Mississippi if her condition did not improve soon. In a town the size of Richland Hills, it would surely make the headline news, as well as the rivaling TV stations if it were to leak out that JoVonna, who was still comatose, lay there, growing a child inside of her, when few people could or would say they had seen her keeping company with a man. JoVonna had once been quoted as saying, "If I pay you, then I certainly don't want to lay with you," and that applied to a lot of the men in Richland Hills and Greenspoint who either worked directly for Rossier Industries or one of its subsidiaries.

Weeks merged into final days before the election and Mayor Brackner sat in his office, his fingers tapping lightly on his plain desk, contemplating the series of facts that would mean he would surely be re-elected to office very soon. His supporters had done a marvelous job of getting the proper amount of exposure for him at opportune moments. His platform was strong and he had been sure all along that he would soundly defeat Larry Booker, his lone opponent.

Since JoVonna never really got the opportunity to officially make it a three-person race, Marcus would slide in. Still, she worried him. Even the fact that she was in the hospital, unable to speak did little to dispel his fears that JoVonna, a woman who thrived on power, and who had proven herself to be a master of unsavory deeds, would eventually return and try to crush him. Marcus had managed, with a great deal of difficulty, to convince Lilly to keep a low profile. He explained that her presence only reminded the whole town of that ugly night almost five months ago that started with a keynote speech, followed by a cat fight and ended the next day with JoVonna Rossier lying comatose in the wing of the hospital she herself had funded at Richland Hills Memorial.

None of the physicians involved in JoVonna's treatment initially suspected a drug-related coma, and even if they had, the narticystozil would not have been readily detectable when mixed with alcohol. The alcohol would have appeared to be the dominant drug, thus leading the doctors back to the conclusion they shared, that JoVonna was a chronic and long-standing alcoholic who was suffering from a prolonged alcohol-induced coma.

JoVonna's Corporation, as well as her other concerns continued to run smoothly. Everyone put forth their best efforts to see that Rossier Industries, a steel-manufacturing corporation ran with maximum efficiency, just the way Ms. Rossier would have it if she were there. Her father's death left her the prime candidate for CEO of Rossier Industries and the board of directors' vote was almost unanimous. She had also gained either a substantial part, or controlling interest in at least three other unrelated companies: A jewelry store, a chain of grocery stores and a small factory that manufactured men's and ladies' clothing in Greenspoint.

On one occasion in the past, minor complications had forced JoVonna to actually go to the clothing factory to sign departmental payroll authorization sheets because she preferred to sign or at least stamp everything that her managers approved. As her employees filed out of the assembly rooms, the humming sounds of the sewing machines coming to a stop combined with the last noises of the steam presses sounded like the end of a song that would tell the story of the people who worked there. For extra money, some of them worked all day, almost every day, and when the day ended, they sometimes appeared too tired to stop. It was as if they came to a stop in slow motion, in perfect tune with the trailing sounds of the machines and presses. JoVonna had positioned herself on top of an oak desk and watched through the glass window of one of the offices as they each appeared at the small window to collect their pay. She would watch them curiously from a distance, wondering what it must be like to be one of them. In her eyes, they would always be inferior, and she wondered why someone did not take away any doubt and tell them that the day they were born.

THE RAIN WILL TELL
Chapter Fourteen

More than six months had passed since the night of the banquet. Marcus Brackner was steadfast in working through the timeline he had set for city improvements during his second term as mayor. The sun was brilliant this breezy morning. The flowers were intoxicating after the rain last evening. As Margot made the last turn down the street to the hospital, she couldn't help but notice that it was lined with crepe myrtle in full bloom. They were caught in the breeze and seemed to be dancing a tango with an invisible partner. Closer to the hospital, the aroma of honeysuckle was nearly overwhelming. Margot stopped in the gift shop to get a paper and fresh flowers for JoVonna's room. She crossed the beautifully appointed atrium and took the elevator up to the suites on the seventh floor, one of which had been JoVonna's home for the past six months.

She opened the door to the suite and began her usual routine of reading JoVonna's medical chart. Her eyes scanned the chart for any new notations. Next, her eyes took in the entire room. She spotted a sheet from a notepad with the ends curled up on a table that listed the dates and times that various members of the press has tried to get a lead on the prognosis for Ms. Rossier. She glanced at JoVonna and amused herself at the thought of what JoVonna might do if she knew what she actually looked like lying there. JoVonna was the kind of woman who took her own measurements very frequently and would throw a whole cake in the garbage if she felt she would not fit perfectly into one of the dresses Raphael designed for her. Somehow now to Margot, JoVonna looked particularly larger from the head to the waist. To the best of her knowledge, JoVonna had not been involved with anyone recently- at least not anyone that she brought to the mansion, so Margot did not even entertain the thought of pregnancy. Still, she thought to herself that

JoVonna looked a great deal fuller than would be caused from bloating, which was the probable cause of weight gain indicated on her medical chart. As Margot turned to straighten her suit in the mirror, she thought she heard a stirring coming from JoVonna's bed but quickly discounted it as her imagination until she turned around just in time to see JoVonna's eyes open, almost as though she had not been comatose for the past six months. Margot stared in disbelief as JoVonna criticized her with her eyes and finally said in very slow, broken sentences,

"Margot.......I told....you....not to ever.....wear that....suit again..... Green is …… awful color on you...you .....look like......well-tailored regurgitated pea soup.

JoVonna's eyes rolled back in her head and she flopped back against her pillows. Margot could only stand there in disbelief, thinking to herself, JoVonna had come back the same hateful, evil woman she was before her accident or illness, whichever it was. When Margot was able to release herself from her temporary state of shock, she nearly turned over everything in her path as she backed out of the room, headed for the nurses' station. As Margot rounded the corner and hurried down the serene, narrow hallway, she slipped and fell, hurting her knee in the process. Two nurses standing nearby helped her to her feet. When she regained her composure, she blurted out, "Ms. Rossier is awake; she is no longer in a coma. Get a doctor in there now!"

Her announcement triggered a barrage of activity. One of the nurses spoke into the intercom, "Calling doctors Mendell and Washington to the central nurses' station, STAT!" The nurses on all shifts had been admonished that if Ms. Rossier did recover, to one, notify the doctors immediately and two, keep the news from the press until a statement was prepared.

JoVonna opened her eyes again, and was trying to pull herself up against the pillows on her bed. She was looking around the suite. One minute, everything appeared clear, and then she would slip back into a haze, with everything in the monochrome room blending and separating. It suddenly dawned on her that she had no idea why she was in the hospital, how long she had been there, or equally as important to her, what kind of toll her stay had taken on her overall appearance. She looked down at her body and let out a blood-curdling scream just as doctors Mendell and Washington rushed into the suite. "There is obviously no atrophy of the esophagus." Dr. Mendell said to Dr. Washington.

"What.... happened.... to.. me?" She screamed at them. She was angry that she could not make her words come more rapidly. "I ..thought.. hospital ..food.. was.. supposed ..to ..be nutritious. I... am ..as.. big.. as ..a ..pregnant.. cow."

"That's the key word, Dr. Mendell responded. Ms. Rossier, we need to have a lengthy conversation."

JoVonna leaned forward, and was immediately reminded of her new weight. She was now aware of her full face and neck, her ample breasts and the bulge in her mid section that refused to let her lean forward to collect a water container from a tray at the end of her bed. She felt embarrassed and unattractive. JoVonna was beginning to complain to her doctors about fluid retention when suddenly, there was a pronounced movement from within her womb, visible to all those present.

"What the hell…..?"

"Ms. Rossier, Doctor Washington began, as he tried desperately to calm her, we estimate that you are just over six months pregnant."

"What… the hell ….are you talking about?"

"Our major concern when you first arrived was your condition at that time. Therefore, it did not fall within the realm of a normal examination at that time to consider pregnancy. Once we determined that there was no brain damage or any other irreparable damage, then we were able to move ahead with a more thorough examination. When we discovered that you were to be a mother, we realized that you might not know yourself, and we went to great pains to keep this information away from the media and the community. We thought it most appropriate for you to communicate this using your own format."

JoVonna's mouth was still wide open, as if it were frozen.

"Is… it …common to have….. memory loss in a….situation….. like this?"

"Yes, very common. Unfortunately, sometimes it's permanent. Why? Do you know of something in particular that you can't remember?"

"No." she lied.

Inside, she was about to go crazy trying to understand how she could possibly be pregnant. She squeezed her eyes shut and focused on the insides of her eyelids where she hoped an image would appear that would clear up this whole mess. She couldn't remember anything past seeing the mayor on stage that night. JoVonna was concentrating so deeply that she did not even hear Dr. Mendell as he tried to direct her attention back to the situation at hand.

"Ms. Rossier, we need to begin a more extensive examination as soon as possible. We need to get you up and on your feet, and even into some therapy to help you regain your normal body functions and to improve your speech and strengthen your motor skills as soon as possible. For the sake of the unborn child, we need to get you on a solid diet as well." JoVonna nodded when necessary, but inside her head was the beginning of a fierce headache because she just could not recall how she got pregnant. Her mind continued to flash back bits and pieces of events right up to very night of the mayor's banquet, but she drew a total blank after that. JoVonna blurted out in what was still somewhat thick garb into the attentive faces of the doctors, "Who knows--- about this--- the baby?"

"As we explained earlier, not a soul knows about your situation. The only regular visitor has been Margot DuPrie and she has purposely been led to believe that this is the result of fluid retention and lack of exercise."

"Where is Margot?" JoVonna inquired. While Dr. Mendell made notations of what tests he wanted run, Dr. Washington walked over to the door and looked out, trying to locate Margot. He walked up to the nurses' station to request that Margot be paged and found that area of the hospital to be buzzing with the news about JoVonna that had now progressed into partial truth and partial preconceived rumors and speculation.

The nurses gathered around Dr. Washington like newborn puppies drawn to their mother, each pushing and shoving for their own tidbits of information. The sound of the stainless steel medical chart cover that Dr. Washington had been carrying brought a sudden end to all the commotion when it hit the counter. "Now that I have your attention, let me first remind you that this is a hospital. Secondly, we are all professionals and must act accordingly all the time."

The nurses stood there silently, waiting for Dr. Washington's next words; each of the nurses had a different agenda. Some of them had truly come to care for Ms. Rossier and were actually relieved that she had started her recovery process. Others wondered how much a newspaper would pay for the abstract details they had managed to gather, but feared divulging that information might be too costly. Still others wished she had died, their hatred for her brimming over as a result of the way she treated relatives or close family members in the past. Dr. Washington left final instructions with the nurses to locate Margot DuPrie.

After Dr. Mendell completed his initial examination, he straightened up and allowed his stethoscope to hang loosely around his neck.

"JoVonna, I am going to re-introduce you to solid foods gradually. Margot told us that you order fresh beef, fish, seafood or poultry from the butcher every day. If you can just bear with us for a while, we'll have you and the child eating steak in no time at all. That last sentence started her head to throbbing again, and her quest to find out who had been in her bedroom the night of the mayor's banquet and what happened after that caused her to break out in a cold sweat. Just at that moment, Dr. Washington re-entered the room and joined in Dr. Mendell's explanation to JoVonna of what they believed happened to her.

"You were fully comatose and your condition was complicated by alcohol. It's no secret that you consume large quantities of alcohol, Ms. Rossier. Your liver tells us your body's history. The morning you were brought in here, your alcohol level was more than two and one half times the level of what is considered a drunken stupor in any state in the union. Above and beyond that, you had the head injury sustained when you hit your head on the bathtub as Margot explained to us. We consulted with a specialist because some traces of a foreign matter were observed but the effects of the alcohol dominated any foreign matter in your system. It appeared to have the same chemical structure or function as high potency sleeping pills, only much more powerful, which when mixed with the amount of alcohol that you had consumed, could have killed you. You and the baby are very lucky to be sitting here today. We had Margot to bring in everything from your medicine cabinet but we found nothing in your home to match what appeared to be a skillfully manufactured coma-enducing drug." Hearing all this served to set JoVonna's thoughts whirling.

"Get.. Margot.. in.. here... now!"

Dr. Mendell opened the door to JoVonna's hospital suite just as Margot pushed from the opposite side. She almost fell again as she entered the room, bearing a bruised knee as a result of her fall earlier in the hallway. With mixed emotions, Margot walked slowly over to JoVonna's bed. She had not really wanted JoVonna to die. JoVonna had literally taken her in. Besides, if JoVonna had died, the fact that she had no relatives would mean that the mansion would have

been sold and Margot was not ready to leave the mansion—
not yet. At the same time, she knew that JoVonna's recovery
would mean that her own life, including her new
independence would be nothing short of miserable.

"Excuse... us... please.... doctors," JoVonna said in a
still somewhat thick and muffled dialect.

As they left the room, JoVonna's disapproving eyes
scanned Margot from head to toe and she was forced to
ponder why she had just run down the hall to get help.

"What... the.... hell... happened.. to me?"

Margot felt an urgent need to summarize all that she
needed to say in as few words as possible and be done with
it. Her words came out jumbled and incomplete - "I don't
really know--not real sure- I found you and your head--"

"Get….. out…. of here!… And don't…. you come
back until you can find, borrow… or steal ..every…
newspaper article, society page or freelance….. effort that
might give me… a clue as to what is ….going on. I want
copies of the newspapers that have followed this debacle…
from the…. day I was brought……..in here until now."
JoVonna had to stop to clear her throat. "Bring me my
damned mail and everything else." Margot instinctively
knew that "everything else" meant she had to find a way to
sneak alcohol into the hospital. She hated that. "Sure, okay."
Margot replied. Tears stung the rims of her eyes as she
momentarily thought about how dedicated she had been to
JoVonna, sticking by her side through all of this, and now,
things were starting up again just as they had left off. The
need for revenge almost choked Margot. She had been good
to JoVonna. Margot pulled the door open by its handle and
turned to look back at JoVonna.

"Is there anything else?"

"There…….. most…. certainly is. You can…. keep
your damned mouth shut about everything you found out
today!"

The room appeared to be spinning to JoVonna as her thoughts began to overlap. She thought to herself, and those thoughts dictated her erratic actions. She pulled at her hair while trying to recollect what happened to her, or better still, what she would tell the doctors the next time they inquired about the drug they had found in her system. She had no idea how it got there, nor did she know who had slept with her about six and one half months ago and why she couldn't recall any of it. The whirlwind in her head that was aimlessly tossing her thoughts around was temporarily interrupted. The mystery guest that had taken up housekeeping inside her body gave her a kick that felt as though the baby was re-arranging her organs to suit its needs. She stared at her swollen belly with a mixture of astonishment, curiosity and anger. When the kicking subsided, she tried once again to focus on the answers to her questions and to the questions the doctors and the entire community would surely have. JoVonna hated being there in that hospital bed in unfamiliar surroundings. She began to associate the fact that she could not remember certain things with the fact that she was stuck here in this hospital suite instead of the comforts of her home. She reached for a pad and pen to make a list of the things to be done before she would be able to go home. She intended to leave the hospital as soon as possible.

JoVonna detested the fact that the town of Richland Hills would have to see her in this condition, but she had to go public and give them the story she wanted them to know before they started to speculate, or even worse, before the man who had been in her bed that night decided to come forth with some gruesome details. JoVonna immediately knew of two things she had to attend to. One, she had to prevent being blackmailed by someone who might have some details about her situation and two, she had to get her story out before someone came forth with details that she could not refute. Her thoughts crowded each other, each presenting itself as a priority, and there was no closure; no way for any of these thoughts to escape, as they still remained unresolved. Mental fatigue pulled JoVonna into a fitful and restless sleep.

Several weeks had come and gone since nature released JoVonna from her comatose state, and since that time she had been poked and prodded and examined and taken to therapy twice daily and finally treated to a complete makeover and silk pajamas, all in an effort to make her feel better about her stay in the hospital.

Margot finished the last of her research and gave JoVonna newspapers with almost every account of what had happened that night more than seven months ago, and every comment or speculative report that she had heard since.

JoVonna insisted that the hospital not include all of the details relating to her admission and subsequent stay in the hospital in the statements they released to the press. She wanted the people of Richland Hills to know as little as possible because she intended to do her own investigation into what had happened to her. She lay there reading every article from several months ago, concentrating on the details until finally she came upon the following article:

The City Of Richland Hills celebrated its Annual Mayor's Banquet on last evening. JoVonna Rossier, CEO of Rossier Industries and owner of a number of other companies was the keynote speaker for the spectacular event for Richland Hills' socially elite. Midway through her speech, Ms. Rossier accused the mayor of disregarding the City Charter and the authority it afforded him. Rossier attacked his morals and accused him of indiscretions. Witnesses say a terrible fight ensued between Ms. Rossier and Lilly Parker, who is said to be the woman the mayor will ask to become his wife. Ms. Rossier was reported to be kicking and fighting while screaming about running for mayor as she was being escorted to her car. She drove away, and at the printing of this edition, no one has heard another word from her.   Meanwhile, another altercation brewed between the mayor and his intended fiancée. They reportedly exchanged several words, and the mayor rushed to his car and was believed to have been spotted later that evening drinking heavily at a bar just outside of town. We are told that the mayor was not in his office the next morning and in fact has not made an appearance anywhere.

JoVonna's eyes lit up and her face began to glow when she finished reading the article. "It was Marcus!" She yelled out loud. Finally, the pieces had come together. She reached for a pad and pen and began to write down what she was thinking. She laid her head on her pillow and began to laugh, saying aloud, "Marcus, you fool! I am finally going to get what I have wanted all along."

JoVonna put the newspaper down and reached over her huge prelude to motherhood for the telephone. It irked her that Raphael's telephone rang three times and he still had not answered. Finally he picked up the receiver and with pins balanced between his front teeth, he managed to blurt out his promo -" Raphael's Custom Designs."

"Oh, enough of that crap. How soon can you see me?"

"I beg your pardon, Raphael replied."

"And I pardon your damned begging." JoVonna retorted.

"Who is... - JoVonna?

"Exactly, and I need to see you now."

"But… but, I heard you were still in the hospital. We were all so pleased to learn that you were recovering."

"I am still in the hospital, but I am going home in a few days and I want something to wear."

"You want me to design a gown for you to wear home from the hospital?"

"No, you Neanderthal, but I do have a special need. I need something airy, with a little room in it."

Raphael scratched the back of his balding head as he thought about the direct contrast to what JoVonna had just requested. Normally, she would throw a dress back in his face if it were not perfectly fitted to her twenty-two inch waistline. Now she was asking for something roomy.

"Well, perhaps I'd better come to the hospital and bring over some drawings. Then we can decide what you'd like me to whip up for you."

"Fine. Raphael, can you be here in one hour?"

"Thirty minutes for you, Darl - uh - Ms. Rossier."

JoVonna placed the phone in its cradle and began to hum a tune as she walked into the bathroom and turned on the shower. It had taken her some time to grow accustomed to her big body, but today she took a long look in the full mirror on the back of the bathroom door at her round belly and full breasts. She smiled to herself at the thought that she had almost effortlessly solved the mystery of who her child's father was. The steam from the shower tempted her and she laid her hairbrush down and climbed in and let the water sound out aquatic rhythms on her body. She dressed in the large emerald green pajamas that Margot had purchased and returned to the bed to close her eyes and rest as she waited for Raphael to arrive.

Raphael selected several fabrics along with some of his most recent sketches. He stepped into his lizard slippers and loaded the items into his BMW and then returned to his shop to make sure he had not forgotten anything before leaving. He brushed his hair into his familiar whirley-bird style. The drive to the hospital was short and uneventful. Raphael reached for the portfolio that contained his drawings and his fabric samples along with the leather case that contained his tape measure and other sewing needs. He stopped to smell the scented flowers in the atrium and then crossed over to the elevators. He felt awful because he had not seen JoVonna in such a long time, but he found out along with all others who had come to see her for various reasons that she was to have no visitors. He picked a fresh flower from the huge pot that sat just outside the elevator. Raphael smelled the flower and stood for a moment examining it, comparing it to his own gardens that flourished annually. He stuck it in the lapel of his suit. He rounded the corner to JoVonna's hospital suite and swung open the door. She opened her eyes and toyed with the covers on her bed. A minute later she threw back the covers and asked,

"Well, what have you got to fit this?"

"Holy Mother of Jesus!"

"Not exactly, but I need some maternity clothes anyway." she retorted.

Raphael's mouth could have served as a tunnel for a freight train as he stood there, both hands on hips, with his tongue resting just slightly behind his lower teeth.

When he could speak, he rattled off a seemingly endless succession of questions.

"Who knows? How far along are you? Who fathered the little..." Raphael stopped short when he realized how personal his questions had become.

JoVonna answered. "No one knows outside of this hospital but you, and it dammed well better stay that way until I get out of here in a week or so.

Raphael stood there as though the floor had turned to quicksand and was slowly pulling him into another place. He couldn't believe she was pregnant.

JoVonna snapped her fingers and said, "Look Raphael, I am paying you by the garment, not by the hour, remember? So far, you haven't earned a dime, so let's get started."

Raphael walked over to where JoVonna had pulled herself up and was standing beside the hospital bed. He laid out the swatches of materials he brought with him, and fearing that he would upset her, he slipped the drawings of the figure-revealing outfits back into his portfolio. He started the awkward task of charting all new measurements for her while she decided on colors. Raphael completed the last of his notes and was packing away his tape measure when there was a light tapping on the door and Margot walked in. She was purposely wearing one of the outfits JoVonna has passed on to her to avoid confrontation. Raphael immediately recognized his work and complimented her on how well the garment fit as he left the room. He turned to tell JoVonna he would be back the following Tuesday and the door closed slowly behind him.

Margot set the fresh flowers she brought on the table beside JoVonna's bed and pulled out a folder that contained some documents JoVonna had asked her to have her attorney prepare.

JoVonna put it aside and looked Margot squarely in the face.

"How long have you known?"

"I suspected that there was more to it than just the fact that you were retaining fluids and not exercising. It just became more obvious as the months went by.

"Did you speak to anyone about your suspicions?"

"Not a soul."

"Good. I have just about completed a statement for the press when the doctors release me next Wednesday. I know that everyone wants to know the details, and because I am such a public figure, I suppose the community deserves to know some of the particulars regarding my plans.

"Did you bring the reports I asked for?" JoVonna checked the list she had been making. "Did you see to it that the papers were typed to revoke power of attorney and proxies for my holdings?"

"Yes, I did. All of the paperwork is right there in that folder. Your attorneys and the Board Members of Rossier

Industries are prepared to speak with you as soon as you either permit visitors, or are released."

"Good, now get out of here and let me get some rest. I plan to resume my regular schedule next week."

Margot turned to look back at JoVonna over her shoulder and then left the room.

THE RAIN WILL TELL
Chapter Fifteen

JoVonna's name was on the lips of at least one or two persons in just about every business, restaurant or social gathering point in Richland Hills, Mississippi. Everyone knew that she was being released from the hospital Wednesday and that she would give a statement at that time. Speculation varied about what she would have to say. The mayor and Lilly sat in a restaurant on the north side of town, and the news about JoVonna being released from the hospital Wednesday annoyed them like a fly practice landing on someone's face on a hot summer day. They spoke softly amongst themselves, loving each other with their eyes and assuring one another that surely there was nothing JoVonna could do at this late date to ruin Marcus' career. After all, he had already been re-elected and his approval rating was steadily climbing with each set of issues he addressed. Marcus patted Lilly softly on her hand and got up to take her home. The question of why he had not asked this fine lady to marry him was also a topic of conversation, and only he knew that he intended to address that issue on the day before JoVonna was being released from the hospital.

Bessie was busy pulling weeds out of the garden that was home to her turnip greens and okra when Willie Mae walked over with a fresh pitcher of lemonade.

"Bessie, what you 'spose that woman up to now? She done woke up. You 'spose we ought to have us a meetin'? It won't be long fore she be comin' back 'round here tryin' to git us to sign somethin'."

"Chile, I don't know." Willie Mae sighed, "She done had folk do a lot of things to us. That child is meaner than the devil hisself. Satan done throwed the cloak of sickness over her all these months and now she done found a way around that. I think we needs to sleep with one eye on that house up there on that hill all the time. I know one thing for sho, we best get out this rain afore we catches pneumonia an' dies an' saves Miss JoVonna the trouble of tryin' to git rid of us huhsef."

THE RAIN WILL TELL
Chapter Sixteen

The residents of Richland Hills awoke to a clear and crisp day after a pounding rain the night before. The event for this day was JoVonna's release. She had gotten up long before the media arrived with their cameras and microphones. JoVonna ordered a huge breakfast and nearly gagged as she did every morning because she would have very much preferred a stiff drink with breakfast. Her beautician finished her hair and after JoVonna admonished her not to speak a word about the pregnancy, she put her out. JoVonna selected a royal blue two-piece suit. The top had been designed to look like a cape, with a stiff neck and two large buttons at the neckline with deep pockets on both sides at hip level. The pencil skirt had a maternity panel but fit snugly, stopping just below the knee, with a delicate slit in back. She slipped into matching leather shoes that caused her swollen feet to protest. JoVonna adjusted her hat carefully and picked up her gloves.

She looked around the room for the last time and let the door close slowly behind her. She found Margot at the business office signing papers and making arrangements for her release. Flanked by nurses, JoVonna headed for the elevator to speak to the press. It was customary for patients to be escorted to the parking area in a wheelchair and JoVonna protested that strongly and won. In her mind, it conjured up an image of weakness and that, compounded with her pregnancy, she did not need. She intended to be back in her office the following day. For now, she concentrated her efforts on what she would say when the cameras greeted her on the ground floor. She had put the facts together in her mind and she now had a statement to make that would be even more scandalous than her keynote address. This statement was going to shock the hell out of Richland Hills, Mississippi.

Marcus awoke early that Wednesday morning and hummed as he dressed, knowing what wonderful plans he had for the day. He checked his appearance in the mirror as he went to open the door for Lilly. He kissed her and rested his hands on her behind at the same time. When she finally ended their kiss by mimicking someone trying to come up for air, he laughed and picked up the tray that he had prepared with hot coffee, fresh fruit and croissants. He and Lilly went out the back door and took the path made of round stones that led to the gazebo in his back yard. Marcus sat the tray down and as Lilly reached out to pour the coffee, the morning sunlight danced on the perfect, one-carat diamond that Marcus had presented to her the evening before.

They had gone dancing, and Marcus invited Lilly over for a cup of coffee afterwards. Marcus carefully took two coffee cups down from the shelf and looked into one attentively. He turned to Lilly and asked, "What do you do when you find a ring in your cup?" Lilly laughed and told him to let the cup soak in a little bit of soapy water and then to clean it out with a soft brush. Marcus looked at her with the innocence of a small boy and said, "I don't think that will work with this ring. I think we need to do something else." Knowing that dish soap and a brush was usually all that was needed to remove a ring, Lilly stood up and walked over to where Marcus was looking down into the cup and reached for it while asking him, "Just what do you suppose we need to do about getting the ring out then?" She looked into the cup and giant tears rolled down her cheeks as Marcus took the exquisite diamond ring out of the cup and said, "I think I should propose with this ring." They spent a glorious night together, and now they sat there in Marcus' gazebo, looking over the rims of their cups at each other and smiling. Anyone looking directly into either of their faces could almost read the story that would tell the entire passionate agenda they shared the evening before. Marcus massaged Lilly's hands. Her thoughts drifted back to the evening before.......*Lilly's favorite song played in the background. The expensive bottle of champagne he surprised her with sat empty on the nightstand next to the bed......"Marcus, baby please, make love to me now!" She begged in between passionate kisses. He tilted her face up to where she could see his and winked at her. "Please Marcus, make love to me." she said again. Instead, he had gently held both of her hands above her head with one of his hands and tempted her between her thighs with the other. He took her nipple in his mouth and savored it like delicious candy ....* Each of them registered the same thought–that they would very much like to start up again where they had left off last night.

The sudden rain shower seemed to offer the reason they needed. They quickly gathered the dishes and ran back to the house. Marcus grabbed two large towels from his bathroom. "We'd better get out of these wet clothes." he said. He walked over to the other side of the room where Lilly was standing and handed her a towel. They both stood there for a moment, watching the local news on the television that sat on a stand in one corner of his living room. Marcus had teased Lilly in the past about being such a news hound. She usually watched the news while he read and smoked his pipe, but today, he wanted her to focus her undivided attention on him. Marcus noticed the handle of a brush just inside Lilly's purse. He picked it up and started to brush her hair. Lilly purred her appreciation and Marcus continued to brush with one hand while he reached around her with the other, his hands becoming entangled in the lacy folds of her blouse while he sought to undo the buttons. Marcus slipped his hand under her skirt and skillfully maneuvered his way past her garter belt. Lilly's body became a slow, smoldering fire. Marcus guided Lilly as she walked backwards over to the settee, dropping the brush in his excitement. He wrapped her legs around him and she ended up in a position where she could see the television, but she had been totally oblivious to what was going on until the cameras focused on the sign that read Richland Hills

Hospital, a limousine and finally JoVonna Rossier standing just outside the two main doors to the hospital.

Lilly's eyes bulged. JoVonna had been in the hospital all this time and yet, there she stood, very obviously pregnant. *What kind of stunt what she trying to pull now?* Lilly thought. While still trying to get over the shock of seeing JoVonna pregnant, Lilly admitted to herself- but would not have said aloud- that JoVonna looked radiant in her maternity suit. *How many people would hire a hairdresser to come and fix their hair while they are in the hospital?* She wondered to herself. Motherhood agreed with JoVonna. Lilly had never been particularly envious of JoVonna before but she found herself flinching now, and she was certain it had nothing to do with Marcus' ongoing efforts. JoVonna Rossier and her pregnancy had managed to capture Lilly's complete attention. Lilly was certain that nearly everyone in Richland Hills was tuned in as well. She tried to tell Marcus what was on television but Marcus swallowed up her words with kisses. He was caught up in the moment and never even recognized JoVonna's voice on the television. He assumed that Lilly had stopped moving because the awkward position they were in had made her uncomfortable, so he shifted one of her legs and begged her to meet him in his efforts. Marcus was beyond anticipation as he tried to change Lilly's position so that her body would give him what he needed. Lilly's eyes and her attention were focused squarely on JoVonna and what she was saying. Marcus had completely removed Lilly's skirt now and added it to the growing pile of clothing on the floor. One of the reporters indicated that JoVonna was prepared to make a statement and all cameras focused on Miss Rossier. She responded to several questions with "I feel great. It's back to business now, and you will know soon enough." A hush fell on those present as JoVonna began.

"As you all are quite aware, almost eight months ago, I had to be rushed to the emergency room of this hospital as a result of the spineless and cruel tactics of the man you foolishly re-elected. You all know how the evening concluded to the public eye, with he and I having a confrontation at the mayor's banquet when I exposed him. What you don't know is that your mayor left the banquet that evening with evil intentions. Witnesses have reported that they saw the mayor having several drinks on that evening. The reason no one saw him after that is because he came to my home, under the pretense that he wanted to sort things out. When the opportune moment arose, he put some sort of chemical in my drink. After the drug had taken effect, he had his way with me, and the result is that I now carry your mayor's bastard child. I will be filing formal charges against the mayor immediately." With that, JoVonna turned and walked directly toward her waiting limousine, waving off all other questions. Reporters tried frantically to get more details but she simply shooed them away with the leather gloves in her hand. Margot got in the car. She was too stunned to speak.

Lilly and Marcus had long since stopped making love. They were now engaged in an all-out, two-person war as Lilly put her clothes back on. She threw Marcus' clothes at him but he refused to get dressed.

"You are a lying bastard."

Marcus reached out and grabbed Lilly's hand mid air as it came within inches of his face. "You told me that after you took me home on the night of the banquet that you had several drinks but you managed to get home. Now I find out right in the middle of you screwing me that you went to see JoVonna that night and screwed her. Well, *screw you*, Marcus!" He could not get a word in edgewise. Lilly snatched up her shoes and purse and stopped at the door. Her eyes were already starting to turn red from salty tears as she glared at Marcus. "It serves you right that she got pregnant when you went tipping over there to sleep with the town's prized and precious "catch". Now you are stuck with her and she will probably drive you out of town right along with everyone else she is trying to get rid of. Did you forget how powerful that bitch is? She will probably have the police rifling through your home and office before the day is over." Lilly threw her engagement ring at Marcus and watched as it bounced off his forehead and rolled onto the floor. She slammed the door. Marcus turned off the television so that he could try to think. He was angry with himself about everything that happened on the night of the banquet. He should have just stayed at Lilly's house that evening. Then there would have been no questions and no doubt. He drank until he fell asleep.

Councilmen Glen Boyd and Bill Henderson knocked on Marcus' door at 5:00 a.m. the next morning. "Are you ready to go fishing?" Glen asked as he stepped into the light so that he could see better. "Damn, where is the truck that ran over you, Marcus?" Both men looked around the room at the uneaten food, the smashed beer cans and the 8 x 10 picture of Marcus and Lilly that had been turned face down. They said simultaneously, "woman troubles." Bill tried to ease the tension by teasing Glen. "Come on, Marcus. Let's go out to the lake and catch some big trout. It will take your mind off things for a while. We can wrap them in the section of the paper where Glen writes his poetry. "Now, let's see, how did that poem go again? "Roses are Nature's ladies, fragrant and…." Glen elbowed Bill. "All I am saying is that any man who writes poetry should expect to take some teasing for it." Bill sidestepped Glen's playful jabs. Marcus shook his head and smiled, but declined to go fishing. Bill turned around at the door.

"Marcus, do you want to talk about it?"

"No. I just need to clear my head. I have to go to the police station this morning."

THE RAIN WILL TELL
Chapter Seventeen

The limousine turned into the circular drive in front of JoVonna's mansion and the clang from the security gate was carried into the southern winds. JoVonna had been nursing a sterling silver flask she kept in her purse. Once inside the house, she had Margot take inventory of the liquor supply. She picked up the telephone and dialed her office. Shirley answered- always by the second ring- as JoVonna had instructed her, "Good Morning, Rossier Industries."

"Get me a list of all pending acquisitions and financial capabilities statements. I want the telephone log for the past eight months. I want minutes from every board meeting this year and a list of all my managers' names in alphabetical order. Include a list of every decision they made that either generated or depleted revenues by more than ten thousand dollars in the past eight months. Get in touch with my accountants and have them in my office at 9:00 tomorrow. I want all of the documents I asked for on my desk at 7:30 sharp." JoVonna hung up the phone and Shirley reached into her drawer for her aspirin. Shirley thought to herself, *The Bitch is back!* She stared at the list JoVonna had barked out moments earlier. Shirley got busy making preparations for JoVonna's return.

News spread throughout Rossier Industries and very quickly throughout her other holdings that JoVonna would be back on her throne the following morning. Rumors from the statement that JoVonna made spread just as quickly, and Shirley about fell over dead when she heard that JoVonna was soon to enter the ranks of motherhood. There was conversation in the office about whether or not JoVonna would continue to drink as heavily as she had in the past. Margot wondered the same thing as she rounded the corner just in time to hear the last of the instructions that JoVonna was giving to Shirley. JoVonna picked up a bottle to fill a glass just as her unborn child decided to make its presence known for the day. JoVonna hesitated as the series of movements took place inside her and then continued to consume the contents of the glass. She went to her bedroom suite and changed into a powder blue silk robe.

Margot was busy with the list of things JoVonna had yelled out to her on the way to her suite. She wrote out a list of meats for the butcher and called a cleaning service. Then she called Raphael's shop and asked him to have someone bring over JoVonna's new wardrobe that consisted of everything from business suits to tailor-made maternity robes.

JoVonna returned to the kitchen and picked up a bowl of fresh strawberries off the counter and went to her library. When it came to her efforts prior to the night of the banquet, it was as though she had never been away. The large portrait of her parents hanging on the wall re-energized her. She methodically picked up her binoculars and focused in on the families with renewed vigor and disdain. The year before, she paid to have all of the acreage surrounding her mansion sprayed for insects. The poison ran downhill and seeped over and killed off the community gardens that the families had joined forces to plant along the fence. The vegetables they sold at various markets were a primary source of income for many of the families. She hoped that would cause them to leave, but she noticed now that each of them had established gardens in their own yards, much closer to their homes and away from the huge fence JoVonna had erected to make sure they always knew where their land ended and what she had declared to be hers began. She looked over on her desk where a copy of a petition lay that she had prepared to try to keep the residents of Richland Hills from having to pay any taxes that might be used to enhance any of the land they owned. She contended that theirs was a private community within Richland Hills and that they should collect their own taxes, build their own sidewalks and even pay for their own sanitation and city services. Her petition was countered with a letter from their attorney. He admonished her that the city of Richland Hills had collected taxes from those families for as long as they had been there, and if she did not consider it a "dead issue" he would go to court and take action against her. JoVonna yawned. She did not like the fact that her body now commanded her to rest, nonetheless, she had to succumb to her heavy eyelids, an indicator that she needed to rest, for herself and for her child.

Bessie and Willie Mae sat on Bessie's front porch as a small group of children played games with homemade toys in the front yard. Willie Mae leaned forward and burned more old bread in her cast iron skillet in her ongoing efforts to keep the flies away. They shared a pitcher of cold water and looked into the distance to where JoVonna's mansion seemed to take on her personality and glare at them. "Word come back from the market she be back in there. Wonder what we can 'spect out o' huh now?" Bessie pondered aloud as she parted her hair down the middle and twisted the gray and black thickness into little buns on each side of her head.

THE RAIN WILL TELL
Chapter Eighteen

Nearly the entire town responded to the press conference that provided a format for JoVonna to proclaim what she had devised as the sequence of events that took place on the evening of the mayor's banquet eight and one half months ago. The news had pitted man against man, woman against woman and group against group. Some came to the immediate defense of the mayor while others argued that he was a man, and that JoVonna was a very beautiful, very desirable woman. There were comments about how proud the mayor must have felt about sleeping with JoVonna, that is, until he got caught, and still others that firmly believed that the mayor would not betray his morals, nor would he be unfaithful to Lilly. There was only one person who knew what really happened, and that person never said a word to anyone about anything involving JoVonna. Instead, the next step in the carefully prepared plans was to wait patiently- always listening and always knowing.

Marcus had been living in a haze since the day JoVonna made the statement that caused the woman he loved so dearly to sever their relationship. Lilly had been humiliated and embarrassed again and that had given her the strength she needed to shut Marcus out of her life. She refused to talk to him and each time after she heard his voice on the other end and slammed the phone down, she would run to the bathroom to be sick and cry until her eyes puffed and stung. Her head ached and her loins desired him. Since the fight, she found herself sleeping with a pillow hugged to her chest. Still, it was no substitute for the smell of Marcus' cologne. When Marcus slept there, he had been so willing to be awakened from a sound sleep to count the stars when she had a restless night.

Lilly owned a small printing company, and she had not been into her office in two days. She sat on the side of her bed making some notes for work and committing herself to go back to the office on Monday morning. Today, Marcus was scheduled to hold a press conference. She sat there, with the television on now, recalling what JoVonna said in her press conference and Marcus' inability to defend himself. She could feel herself growing angry again. As the minutes ticked away until Marcus' conference, Lilly's thoughts drifted. Marcus and Lilly had fallen in love right away. Lilly knew for a fact that when there was a rumor in Richland Hills, it seemed to be carried from house to house and business to business like some kind of gossip torch. Otherwise, she might have given in to the temptation to invite Marcus to her house for dinner the first time he had come to her shop to discuss a rather large printing job related to his first attempt at campaigning for mayor. Their eyes never left each other and Lilly involuntarily moistened her lips. She had been more than happy to give him her business card along with a look that told him it was fine if he wanted to call her. She remembered the sexy way Marcus winked at her and then turned and walked away. Now, as Lilly sat there, her eyes filled up with tears and she hated JoVonna for knowing Marcus so intimately. She hated Marcus for sharing something with JoVonna that she could not get enough of herself.

She opened her eyes, and there sat Marcus with pain seared into his face. Lilly noticed that he wasn't even wearing one of his best suits for television, and suddenly she wanted to be there to straighten his tie and be the wealth of support that she had always been for him. The camera focused first on his office, which was literally bare for a man of his means, then on the interviewer and finally on Marcus. He cleared his throat before he began to speak but his audience could still hear the strain in his voice. Marcus answered a series of questions directed at him with as few words as possible. Most of the town of Richland Hills listened and waited for Marcus to reassure them, to say something to put an end to all the rumors.

"I can assure you that I will be unswerving in my responsibilities as mayor and that all other matters will be handled privately and expeditiously." With that, he beckoned to the cameraman to stop filming. Marcus could not afford to let the town see how distraught he was. He wanted to take shelter within himself. He left the interview and walked into the conference room directly down the hall and gave in to the feelings in his heart and dialed Lilly's number. He knew that if only he could somehow find a way to make her listen to *her* heart that she would have to listen to his words too, and then he could make things between them right again. Lilly turned off the television. She knew it was Marcus when the phone rang, and her heart wanted her to answer, but she refused.

JoVonna watched a while longer to see if Marcus would make an even bigger fool of himself. She laughed, shook her head and turned off her television as she reached for her telephone. She dialed the rotary phone with a pencil and waited.

"Mayor Brackner's office, may I help you?"

"Tell him that the mother of his child is on the telephone."

"He's busy, Miss Rossier!"

"You'd better watch the way you speak to me, young lady, or I'll add firing you to the list of things I have prepared for Marcus to do. Put this call through now!"

JoVonna refilled her glass and munched on an olive while she waited for Marcus to pick up the line. The child inside of her seemed to have been trying out for the Olympics and JoVonna had experienced Braxton-Hicks contractions more than once now.

"This is Marcus." The voice sounded like it was all that was left of a drained man. JoVonna yawned into the telephone and then started interrogating Marcus.

"Well, mayor, what are your plans for this bastard child?" Marcus sighed heavily into the receiver. "JoVonna, I love Lilly. I don't want to have a damned thing to do with you, your child or your life, period."

"Well, I'll just have to--"

"Listen, you caviar-eating bitch, you have practically ruined my life. You can take your threats and go to hell."

"So, are you telling me that you still have no balls when it comes to those people? Are you saying that I have to expose our child to that bad element? Marcus, it's obvious that you will never fill a real man's shoes, so whose apron strings are you going to hold onto now?"

"Fuck you, <u>AND</u> the horse you rode up on!" Marcus shouted. He hung up the telephone and felt a little uneasy, wishing for Lilly at a time when JoVonna had just taunted him about apron strings. Marcus had a brilliant thought. He picked up the telephone and called Richland Hills Hospital.

"How may I direct your call?"

"The maternity ward, uh...delivery, Nurse Brenda Billford, please.

"One moment."

"This is Nurse Billford."

"Brenda, this is Marcus. How are you?"

"I'm fine, Marcus. How are you getting along? We all heard the news about you being, well, uh." She cleared her throat. "We heard what JoVonna said on television about you fathering her child."

"Well, that's exactly what I want to talk to you about. Can I meet you in the park across from the hospital in about fifteen minutes?"

"Sure Marcus, anything for you." She hung up the telephone and envied both Lilly and JoVonna momentarily as she thought about the man she was about to meet in the park. According to rumor, both women knew him intimately. Brenda could only imagine what a night with him might be like. Marcus was perfect in her eyes. He was tall and well built, with a physique that could make an off-the-rack suit look as if it were tailored for him. Brenda thought to herself that this well-dressed southern man was a prize waiting to be unwrapped. Marcus was clean-shaven with gray-blue eyes that seemed to invite you inside his soul to explore the remarkable man that he was. Marcus' hair was thick, dark and obedient. His skin beckoned you to come and know its smooth masculinity. Brenda shuddered and looked down at the diamond wedding ring on her left hand. Pushing away her thoughts, she put away the charts she had been working on and walked through the double doors of the hospital and across the street into the pre-holiday brisk air where Marcus sat waiting for her. He motioned for her to sit down and offered her a cup of coffee. He hesitated at first. This woman had been his friend since high school. Still, he was not quite sure how to ask her for what he needed.

THE RAIN WILL TELL
Chapter Nineteen

JoVonna sat on a chaise lounge in her bedroom suite, intrigued by a story she had come across in a newspaper about two men who had been arrested in connection with the murder of a prominent young woman in Kansas City. The police had not been able to keep the men in custody because there was no evidence. She was distracted from the story because her stomach had become very hard and the child inside of her was very still. JoVonna had started to feel uncomfortable. She placed her hands on either side of her stomach and looked down, trying to imagine what the experience she was about to go through would be like. She knew that there would be some degree of pain associated with her delivery. The team of doctors that had worked to support her throughout her coma and now through her pregnancy had done all they could to prepare her body and her mind for what was about to happen to her now. Her doctor's plea for her to seek help to quit drinking had fallen on deaf ears, and just as he feared, JoVonna would be intoxicated at the time she delivered her child. When the first contraction started, she took a deep breath and tried to maintain her composure. Thirty minutes passed with intermittent contractions, each one a little more intense than the last. She sat there, mouth dry, eyes bulging from fear, trying to gather her thoughts. The pains were closer now.

The lace curtains swayed at the coaxing of the wind coming through the window, reminding JoVonna of how soft they were. The antique bedspread looked as relaxing as a ride on a cloud, yet this room seemed to have turned against her. She felt like the all-white bedroom was closing in on her, squeezing her like a giant white vice, robbing her of her breath. She managed to stand, and when she did, her amniotic fluid sac broke. She felt as if Niagara Falls was coming out of the lower half of her body. She screamed and ran to her bathroom and stood in the bathtub. JoVonna closed her eyes and tried to become the victor in the battle she was having with the alcohol inside her. She felt the need to be sick and to scream at the same time. She screamed and Margot rounded the corner to see what she was yelling about. She was startled at the sight of JoVonna standing there, clutching a bar of soap with one hand and trying to stop Niagara Falls with the other hand. She was soaked with perspiration, and her makeup was ruined.

"Don't you dare just stand there, damn you! Get me out of here and help me to get cleaned up. It's time to o-o-o-o-o-o go have this bastard child, and the sooner I do, the sooner I will have the leverage I need to get rid of those damned----" JoVonna screamed again. Margot managed to get her undressed and seated on a leather vanity stool. She cleaned JoVonna's face and was frantic when JoVonna insisted on trying to reapply her makeup. JoVonna started to scream at her. "Hurry up, damn you! This pain is unbearable!"

Margot slid two gold combs on either side of JoVonna's hair and pulled the phone by its cord to the bathroom. Her fingers seemed to freeze and stubbornly conformed to the holes as she used the rotary phone to call JoVonna's doctors.

"Richland Hills Hospital, how may I direct your call?"

"I need to speak with Dr. Mendell. I have an emergency."

Moments seemed like an hour to JoVonna, who had thrown her makeup on the floor. "Where is the damned doctor?" She had asked Margot the same question twice before doctor Mendell answered the call.

"Mendell speaking."

"Doctor Mendell, this is Margot DuPrie. Ms. Rossier is ready to have the baby. Her contractions are starting to become regular and her amniotic fluid sac has broken. "

"Get her to the hospital now. We'll be waiting."

Margot put JoVonna's arm around her shoulder to lend her the strength she needed to make it to the Cadillac. JoVonna had started sweating some time ago. Her clothes were clinging to her now. Perspiration ran down her face and matted her hair. JoVonna had never even imagined pain or discomfort like this and it infuriated her that she was not in control of her body. Her thoughts were temporarily distracted between contractions as she thought about the community within a community. She tried to take her mind off the pain by thinking about the lawsuit she would file contending that those families had damaged a fence that she had erected to make sure no more of them managed to wander up on her property. Pain interrupted her thoughts. When she could focus again, JoVonna remembered that she had waved off with a flick of her wrist the fact that the surveyor had informed her that she had far exceeded the boundaries of her property line and that the fence was definitely erected on their land. The thunderous pains in her belly brought her back to the realization that she was indeed in her employee's car being rushed to the hospital to have what she figured to be her key to the city and the solution to finally getting rid of the community within a community–the Mayor's child.

THE RAIN WILL TELL
Chapter Twenty

The doors to the maternity entrance of the hospital swung open and two nurses waited on either side of a wheelchair to lead JoVonna to labor and delivery. While Margot finalized the admitting paperwork, JoVonna sat thinking in between pains, and it dawned on her that she had never even wondered what this child would look like. She thought about the fact that Marcus had dark, chiseled features and she herself had naturally blonde hair that cascaded down her back, stone-mountain blue eyes, tight skin and an overall appearance that epitomized what half the women in Richland Hills would have gladly paid money to look like. Before she became pregnant, men dreamed about her. She had been an hourglass-shaped fantasy, and now she sat there, watching Margot with her long hair neatly secured with a clasp and her figure still in tact. She hated every woman with a waistline at that moment and vented her frustrations on Margot. When there was a momentary pause in the commotion, JoVonna took advantage of the opportunity to tell Margot that she looked horrible and knew nothing about the fine art of dressing as a lady should. Margot turned around and glared at JoVonna, as did some of the nurses at the station. After another moment, with people staring and showing their discontent for the remark, JoVonna demanded to be taken to her room immediately.

Brenda Billford, who had previously been torn between her oath as a medical professional and being a loyal friend to Marcus, made up her mind at that moment to grant Marcus' request for information.

She found a place that afforded her some privacy to use the telephone and dialed the mayor's number.

"Marcus, this is Brenda. JoVonna is here. It's still going to be several hours, but I will do what you asked."

"Thank you very much, Brenda. That information will be tremendously helpful. We'll talk again soon."

Brenda hung up the receiver and went to JoVonna's room to take her vitals, draw blood and get the intoxicated, first-time mother on course for the long road ahead. The nurses informed Margot that JoVonna would probably be in labor for some time yet to come.

JoVonna had instructed Margot on exactly what to pack in her hospital bag, but when she got to the hospital, she started complaining about a robe and a pair of slippers that weren't there and she wanted another hairbrush. When Margot arrived back at the mansion to pick up the things JoVonna had yelled at her about, she noticed that JoVonna's bed was covered with the suits and dresses that Raphael had created based on her measurements prior to her pregnancy as an incentive for her to work on her figure after the baby was born. Margot cursed under her breath as she started to hang them up and then had a much better idea. It was two days before Christmas. She found a large box in the storage closet and put all the clothes in it. Then she gift wrapped it and fashioned a large red bow out of a roll of ribbon. She wrote a note that said "Merry Christmas to you all" and secured it to the box. She dragged the box to the trunk of the Cadillac and managed to lift it into the trunk. She went to the tool shed for the longest rope she could find. Margot laughed aloud as she drove to where the fence that separated JoVonna's property from the other families had been erected. She tied the rope around the box and threw the loose end over the fence. She climbed the fence and used her rope to pull the large box over the top. The rope caught for a moment, but she gave a hard yank and moved out of the way as the box of clothing fell to the ground, just missing her foot. Margot laughed again as she alternated pulling and pushing the box over to the door at the rear of the church where the community within a community worshiped. She ran the short distance back to the fence, grabbed the rope and climbed over to JoVonna's side of the property as quickly as she could.

Things had taken a change for the worse for JoVonna. She vomited more than once. Nurse Billford called housekeeping to clean the floor and bring JoVonna a clean blanket. Another nurse offered JoVonna ice chips. She threw the cup across the room and began to cry. JoVonna was frustrated and afraid. She had developed a slight fever and trying to get her to dilate past four centimeters was a long, slow process. The doctors conferred amongst themselves, wondering if she would be strong enough to deliver on her own after the recovery from the coma and everything else her body had to contend with. The nurses took her blood pressure every thirty minutes and kept cold compacts on her forehead and cups of chipped ice beside her bed. JoVonna's own alcohol level served as a painkiller, but it was a hindrance as well. It complicated matters and caused the doctors to deny the comforts of anesthesia because they feared her alcohol content might interact with it.

When she finally delivered the small child hours later, there was a period of relief for everyone. The doctors were tired, the nurses were frustrated and JoVonna was glad the child had finished hurting her. Nurse Brenda Billford had taken the baby boy away after the umbilical cord was cut to remove the vortex cream from the infant. She had difficulty clearing his lungs and notified the doctors. His tiny cry was barely heard amongst the doctor's orders for a respirator and other medical procedures. Dr. Mendell busied himself with JoVonna's sutures and nurse Billford took the opportunity to extract an extra vial of blood from the child. She placed the vial in her pocket. When she turned to place the infant in JoVonna's arms, the room was still full of commotion. JoVonna did not appear to be fully coherent and was not lending any cooperation to the situation at hand. Nurse Billford handed the infant to the nurse standing next to JoVonna's bed and walked through the confusion and headed straight for the lab. She pulled out a box that she had hidden amongst several boxes of cotton swabs and opened it. Inside was a copy of a page from JoVonna's hospital chart that indicated what her blood type was and the results from the blood sample she had taken from Marcus earlier. When she finished the test, she noted the baby boy's blood type, took all the documents and cleaned up what she had disturbed in the lab. She walked back through labor and delivery and saw that JoVonna was finally asleep. Brenda called Marcus and asked him to meet her at the park.

Marcus was nervous as he approached Brenda. His whole future hinged on a mistake he might have made the night of the banquet; a mistake he could not even remember.

Brenda looked into his eyes and found herself wanting to kiss him.

"Well?"

"I got the sample and was able to do the test."

Marcus shifted his body on the bench so that he was now directly facing her.

"What was the result, Brenda? What did the test indicate?" Marcus' voice was louder than he intended.

"It's not your baby, Marcus. I ran the test twice and it was conclusive. It is not possible for you to have fathered JoVonna's child. She handed him a sheet of paper. Marcus jumped up and cheered. Brenda laughed at his antics. He pulled Brenda to him and hugged her.

"Thank you, Brenda. You don't know how much this means to me."

"Well, Marcus, it's only fair. No one should have to shoulder the blame for something they did not do."

He was still holding her in his arms.

"You're a special lady, you know that? If there is ever anything I can do for you, just let me know."

He kissed her softly on the mouth and turned and left. Brenda watched him walk away and tried to ignore the warm sensation under her uniform. She crossed the street and returned to the hospital.

Marcus stopped and picked up a bottle of champagne and the ingredients for the best breakfast he knew how to cook. Marcus was elated and he felt like a kid on Christmas Eve. He prepared a splendid meal and put it in a big basket. He timed himself so that at one minute past midnight on Christmas morning, he got out of his car and walked up the driveway to Lilly's house. When she opened the door, they read each other's eyes, each seeing loneliness and desire. Lilly wanted to resist, but her love for him compelled her body to move aside, and she let him in. Marcus set the table without a word and they ate in silence. Marcus tried to make small talk but Lilly was not receptive. More than once he started to just blurt out the news to her, but he was determined to have her receive it gift wrapped. Shortly after they had finished breakfast, Lilly rose and walked over to the front door, making a silent gesture for Marcus to leave. He walked over to where she stood and handed her the gift-wrapped test results.

"What is it?' Lilly asked, more curtly than she had intended.

"Please, just open it."

Lilly refused, and it angered Marcus that he had come so close to resolving this impasse in their relationship and Lilly was thwarting his efforts by refusing to open the package.

"Open the damned package!" Marcus yelled.

Lilly was angry now, and threw the package that contained their future happiness across the room. Marcus wanted to tell her but he was already choking back tears. He grabbed his coat and left. Marcus daydreamed and deliberately took an alternate route home so that he could see Main Street. He slowed down to take in the lights that winked from atop the buildings in the stillness of the early morning. He drove past giant wreathes and illuminated candy canes and as the last of the ambiance of Christmas on Main Street was reflected in his rear view mirror, he wished that Lilly had opened his gift to her. It was cold and gray on this Christmas morning and the clouds were proving to be relentless against the sun, not allowing it to dominate, even for a few minutes.

When Marcus got home, he parked his car in front of his large, wood-framed home. Lilly had chided him about this habit in the past, saying that he always left his garage for his guests. He opened the door, hung up his coat and started to make a fire. Lilly had unwrapped and read the package containing the medical reports shortly after Marcus left. She verbally assaulted herself for being such a fool as she dressed frantically. It was unlike Lilly to leave her house untidy, but today she did not care. She left the breakfast dishes in the sink and snatched dresses out of her closet, looking for the new one that Marcus had told her was sexy. She loved her man and now she was only one high-heel shoe away from being able to tell him that. She hopped towards the door as she put her shoe on. Minutes later, she had deliberately broken the Richland Hills speed limit to beat him back to his house and parked in his garage. She had hidden in his bedroom closet where the smell of his cologne on his clothes made her desire him even more. While Marcus was in the bathroom, Lilly sneaked out to where he had been watching television and turned upright the 8 x 10 picture of the two of them that he had turned face down the day they had the fight that caused her to leave him. When Marcus finished showering, he walked over and stood in front of the fireplace, letting the heat dry him. Towel in hand, he walked over to sit down in his chair. Was it his imagination or could he actually smell Lilly's fragrance? Then he noticed it, - the picture- "She's been here!" Marcus pranced around like a spirited young pony saying over and over again, "She's been here!" When he danced back past his bedroom door, Lilly stood sprinkling baby powder on the sheets.

"I'm still here, baby."

No more words were exchanged. Marcus took her in his arms and kissed her as if he could somehow give her an infusion of his love. He pressed his naked body against hers, and she could feel the heat and hardness of his anticipation. Marcus complimented Lilly on her dress as he unzipped it and watched it fall to the floor. Her hands told him what she wanted. Lilly wore Marcus' favorite fragrance. Marcus explored her body as if it were an exotic fruit. He followed the trail of her perfume down to her parted thighs and tasted her. His hands followed his tongue over the familiar curves of her body. He made love to her until they were almost satisfied, then paused to digest the thought of having this magnificent woman by his side again. Lilly took the lead and sat astride Marcus, taking what she wanted. Marcus surrendered his body to Lilly, matching her movements with upward thrusts. They drifted off to sleep from exhaustion and when they awoke, Marcus made love to Lilly again, more aggressively this time. He had missed her and the way she made him feel. As he reclaimed her body, he whispered to her, begging her to never leave him again. Lilly welcomed him back into her life.

"Merry Christmas, baby."

"Merry Christmas to you too, Marcus."

Lilly went to mix eggnog and brandy and Marcus pulled two robes from his closet. He already had a hot tub running when she returned with the drinks. They thought to themselves how good it was to be together again.

"You know, you could sue the pants right off her holier-than-thou ass for libel, slander and even defamation of character." Lilly said lazily as Marcus shampooed her hair.

"I ran that by my attorney the first day that damned thing aired. He requested a written copy of her statement. He said that she had all of her pronouns in place and that she never actually mentioned my name. Technically, when she made reference to "your mayor", that would have been relative to who was watching the program. She also never mentioned a specific date. What she did turned this town upside down. She is too smart to let herself get entangled in a lawsuit. I don't need the cash anyway, but I'm telling you, there will come a time shortly when I am going to make that woman fall off her high horse. Besides, I have got something in store that will hurt her much more than just losing a little cash." Lilly washed his back and then got out of the tub to heat a towel and get a straight razor so that she could shave him while they continued to talk.

"What do you have in mind, Marcus?" Lilly grinned.

"Why don't we meet for lunch tomorrow and you can help me with my strategy?"

"Okay. What do you suppose she will be up to next?"

"I don't know, but some of the council members have warned me that she has requested a copy of the agenda and some other information about the next quarterly meeting, which is in April. If we wait until then, everyone will be back from holiday vacation, and we can execute our plan without the suspicions that would arise if I call a special meeting. Besides, I don't know if JoVonna would be willing to attend a special meeting, but I am certain she will be at the next quarterly meeting."

"Does she know about the test results?"

"Hell no! She never even asked what the child's blood type was, and even if she had, she doesn't know what my blood type is. Brenda would have–well, let's just say that I made sure that she will go on thinking that I am that kid's father until I want her to know otherwise."

"Okay, honey, but let's start working on the plan now. That is the kind of thing you want to clean up as soon as possible."

THE RAIN WILL TELL
Chapter Twenty-one

It was check out time for JoVonna and her new son. She was in the restroom having a drink from a flask while Margot dressed the child, who had been named Michael George Rossier after JoVonna's father. She rinsed out her mouth in an attempt to be less conspicuous around the doctors and nurses who hounded her to stop drinking. She had tried to stop drinking more than once, but alcohol was her comforter. It kept her warm in her bed at night and took the place of her parents' love.

She picked the child up and awkwardly cradled him in her arms and motioned for Margot to pick up the diaper bag and other gifts from the hospital. She tried to keep as far away from the nurse in the room as possible, fearing that she had not used enough mouthwash to camouflage her habit. When they reached the exit, a sunny but crisp Friday morning greeted the threesome as they headed for the car. As JoVonna watched Margot get the child settled in the car, she began to feel a little uneasy. She had a new son to care for, weight to lose and an entire community to restore to the way she thought it ought to be. The child in the blanket had dark features and JoVonna smiled as she thought about the leverage the child would give her with Marcus.

Margot pulled into JoVonna's reserved parking space at Waltham Towers and they walked the path to the building in silence. Margot thought JoVonna should go home since it was her first day out of the hospital. JoVonna had insisted that when she was discharged from the hospital she would go to her office. Margot called the office and changed the date of the baby shower. They walked towards her personal conference room where the food and gifts were. The greetings were lukewarm, but even her employees who felt the same way about her as Shirley did could not help but to ooooh and aaaah over what they thought was the mayor's baby. No one dared to whisper while JoVonna opened her presents. Instead, they watched as she purposely created two separate stacks. When she had gathered all the items that she wanted, she placed them in the stroller while the others sat and ate ice cream and cake. When she was finished, she took her baby from Shirley. Margot tried to hide her embarrassment as she pushed the stroller out into the hallway. JoVonna told those present that she would be in the office again on Monday morning and then left without another glance at the gifts that she felt were not good enough for her baby and therefore, had chosen to leave behind. When they were in the hallway, Margot turned to JoVonna and said, "You are going to need some of those things you left in there." JoVonna looked her squarely in the face and said, "I have never needed anything in my life that I could not buy or take."

When they got home, Margot took the baby to the nursery she had prepared for him. She began to cook something to eat while JoVonna got settled with a drink to take care of some unfinished business. After a while, she decided to take a break from the paperwork concerning her holdings and take a look at the community within a community. She watched for a while as two of the younger women stood talking, and marveled at how well dressed they were. The more she watched, the more familiar the custom suits became to her. She ran to her suit closet and then back to her binoculars.

"Damn!" she screamed. That two-piece....that silk….. those are my clothes! How in the world did they get– "Margot! JoVonna rounded the corner and went through the formal dining room to the back of the mansion. "Margot, why didn't you notify the police immediately that my home had been burglarized? Why wasn't I told?" Margot placed the baby gently in his wooden cradle and turned to face JoVonna. She bit her lip and managed to say with a straight face, "What are you talking about?"

"Those people are not content to have my land. Now they have been in my home, and I want the police to know about this right now! You can call Marcus and tell him this is what I have been warning him about all along."

Margot struggled to keep a straight face.

"What makes you think that they have been in here?" Margot asked.

"Because they are wearing my clothes. We better check to see what else is missing."

"Oh. Then they probably got them from the Salvation Army."

"And just what would my clothes be doing at the damned Salvation Army?" JoVonna could taste the anger that was building inside her.

"I assumed that's what you wanted done with them when you left them all laying on the bed and on the floor." She swallowed a laugh.

"Well, that's just stupid, Margot. In fact, it starts a new chapter in the novel titled: How To Be Stupid Just Like Margot."

With that, she turned and stormed out of the room, leaving Margot to her secret satisfaction. Margot laughed until her nose ran and her stomach hurt. They were very expensive clothes and she knew it would humiliate JoVonna every time she saw a woman from the community within the community wearing one of her suits. JoVonna was trying her best to take something away from them that she felt should be hers and she certainly did not want them to have anything else.

JoVonna mixed another drink and stood looking down into the cradle at the sleeping child. It was too early to tell what the child would look like, but she felt that in the coming months the child would look so much like Marcus that she would be able to stamp "duplicate" across his forehead.

On her way out to her gardens, she noticed the stack of old newspapers she had been reading before she went into labor beside the door. It had rained several times since Margot placed the papers by the door and the papers were damp and matted now. JoVonna yelled back inside for Margot to have the papers removed and again turned her attention to her gardens. She looked to the partly cloudy sky for assurance that spring was soon to come. JoVonna was impatient for the days when her honeysuckle would blossom again. She looked along the gardens to where it would run its full course and took solace in the fact that soon there would be beautiful azaleas and mums and gardenias. There was a row of trellises that stood along the eight-foot wall behind her mansion and in the spring it would be heavy laden with antique roses. Several yards to her right was a rickety old wrought iron fence that never stayed fastened. Directly through it, a circular drive wound its way from the front of the mansion around and down a steep hill to the four-car parking garage. Her Mercedes sat outside of the garage doors most of the time. At night, floodlights dared anyone to step out of the shadows on this, the only side of the mansion that was not completely protected by the wall. Just on the other side of the garage would soon be the setting for a field of sunflowers and beyond that stood mature oak trees and pecan trees and an old storage shed and stables.

As JoVonna continued to walk, she was reminded of the days when her mother used to pack a lunch and walk out to where she and her father would sit high atop the hill. She stood now and looked down onto the rest of her land. JoVonna and her father used to watch the willowy grass as it seemed to sway back and forth to a tune that only nature knew. As she looked from the top of the hill now, she remembered why she had not come back out this far on her land until now. There, just beyond where the land flattened out, she could see the square outlines that were their houses. She turned away and started back toward her gardens. She finished her third drink and fished in the glass for the olive just as she passed through the gate and back up into her gardens. Mother Nature was unusually kind to Mississippi's townsfolk this afternoon. It was turning into a cloudless day and the sun seemed to warm JoVonna like a light shawl. She was unable to concentrate on the paperwork she had brought home from her office so she sat in a chair near the door.

"Margot, fix another drink for me and then bring the baby out." Margot looked up from where she sat feeding Michael George.

"I think it might be too chilly for such a young child." she replied.

She wanted to tell JoVonna that the alcohol had deceived her and that it was not as warm as she thought it was.

"Oh nonsense. Bring the boy out!"

Margot protested again. JoVonna was angry now and got up quickly from her seat and headed back indoors. As her gait quickened, she tripped over the hem of her robe and fell and hit her cheek on a wrought iron table. Margot stood staring, her mouth wide open as JoVonna got up from the ground and charged toward the mansion. She caught her reflection in the glass door on the way in and could not believe how quickly her cheek started to swell and bruise.

"This is your fault, bitch!" JoVonna said, as she stood flat footed and stared at Margot with a look in her eyes that could have won this battle for her.

"I pay you to do what I say!" she screamed. "Look at my face!" She could feel that her face had started to bleed and she could not stand the idea that Margot stood there, all her composure intact. She saw a fork in the dish drain and snatched it out. JoVonna swiped the fork across Margot's face, surprising and hurting her at the same time. Margot raised her fist and punched JoVonna twice and had a patch of her hair pulled out before she saw the baby's face. She twisted JoVonna around so that she could see the baby's face too.

"Look, dammit! Your son is choking!"

His face was red from crying and his body was still except for his lower lip that seemed to be working desperately at drawing in air. She and JoVonna bumped shoulders like two rams engaged in combat as they passed each other. Margot started to tend to the baby, checking to make sure there was nothing in his mouth. She patted his back lightly. JoVonna took this opportunity to escape from the fight she had provoked. Margot picked the child up and cooed to him.

"I bet your mommy doesn't even know what your feeding schedule is."

As soon as she was sure the child was okay, she put an ice pack on her face to stop the stinging and prevent swelling. Then she went to the medicine cabinet. She took deep breaths to calm down. Fortunately, the scratches were not very deep and they were high on her face. The combination of her hair and skillfully applied makeup would cover them until they healed. JoVonna sat in her office with the door locked drinking and trying to concentrate on some paperwork. She did not know what to expect from Margot. She cracked her door and looked out several times in the next few minutes to see what Margot was doing. JoVonna came across the check that she had written for Margot's bonus and decided to increase it. She knew that if Margot left now that she would be in trouble. JoVonna knew that she would have to apologize to her if she wanted Margot to stay, but decided to put that off as long as possible.

The new year was in its third month now and a rare and fine powdery snow had dusted Richland Hills and lay there, waiting to collect the footprints of all those who ventured out. The tension in the Rossier mansion was still undiluted. Margot cared for the child and ran the house while JoVonna drank and decided to work out of her home for a few days. Michael George Rossier grew rapidly as time passed, and JoVonna was sure that he looked more and more like Marcus.

THE RAIN WILL TELL
Chapter Twenty-Two

Marcus and Lilly had completed plans that called for them to wait until all of the residents of Richland Hills returned from Easter vacation. He didn't want anyone to miss what he had to say. The first week in April, Marcus called JoVonna at her office where she now spent most of her time since there was still so much tension between her and Margot. He waited late enough in the day to ensure that she was alone and would have to answer her own phone. He certainly did not want to stir up any fresh rumors. She answered on the third ring.

"JoVonna Rossier"

"JoVonna, this is Marcus."

"Well, if it isn't the caring and concerned father of my child."

Sarcasm seeped out of her voice, surrounding her like steam. "How very kind of you to call to inquire about your illegitimate son. I spank him when he cries so he won't become a spineless reject from the male species like you. And how is dear Lilly? Is she wishing she had given birth to your first born child instead of me?"

"JoVonna," Marcus said evenly, forcing down his anger. "I did not call to spar with you. Do you still have the proposal on taxing the property that your neighbors live on?"

"Yes, I do, but—"

"Do you have anything else?" he interrupted.

"Well, I have some notes that I have taken recently. I had several more, but I cannot seem to find them. Did you take them the night you were here, preferring me to Lilly?" JoVonna laughed. "Is that why you are going to get rid of those leeches after all this time? Do you want to sleep with me again, Marcus?"

Marcus had to discipline his tongue to keep from telling her what he knew right then and there.

"Would you just compile all that information and . bring it to my conference room on Thursday morning at 9:00?

"Isn't that when the Council meets?"

"Yes, they will be there as well."

"What are you planning, Marcus?"

"To settle some issues once and for all."

"I'll be there." JoVonna responded. "I'm glad you're finally coming to terms with the problems those people have caused."

JoVonna paused for a moment. "Would you like to see– would you like me to bring your son?"

Marcus was surprised by the question, and it served to reinforce just how important it was for him to resolve the whole issue.

"No." Marcus said. There will be too much going on. This could be long and drawn out. That would not be good for the baby."

"Why Marcus, do I detect a note of concern?"

JoVonna smiled and Marcus grimaced at the same time.

He hung up the phone, as did JoVonna. Lilly put down the extension and smiled at Marcus. "She bought it."

Lilly walked over to him and kissed him lightly on the forehead. "JoVonna still does not have a clue."

"That's right." Marcus said as he wrapped his arms around her and took the pearls that she wore around her neck between his teeth. "And you don't have a clue what I have in mind for you." Lilly leaned back, looked at the man she was in love with and gave him her best smile. They left his office some time later and stopped for a bottle of Chardonnay on the way back to his house. Marcus made a small fire to take the chill out of the air. He stopped momentarily to gauge his

106

wood supply against the remaining cool days left to come and decided that he would not need to cut more wood. Lilly busied herself making a green salad, beef tips and homemade mashed potatoes seasoned with garlic, pepper and butter. She set out custard that she had made earlier. Marcus set the table and put out the wine. They discussed his plan for the upcoming Thursday. Marcus told Lilly that he was going to enjoy being the one to knock JoVonna off her high heels and apologized again for being so inebriated the night of the banquet that he could not remember if he had been with JoVonna or not. Lilly put her finger to his lips to silence him. "Marcus, we have loved each other past that. Let's focus on your plan."

JoVonna hoped to use the child to tap into Marcus' sympathy, but he intended to stop her dead in her tracks on Thursday. He and Lilly finished dinner, and Marcus squeezed Lilly to him and kissed her forehead. "Get some rest." he whispered. "We've got a lot ahead of us." He kissed her again more passionately and went to get her coat.

Despite the rain, Richland Hills continued to function as a small town with weekly rituals. The women, with hats and gloves as standard attire–at least those with husbands to support them, would meet over on Copperwood Street. They admired the displays in the small shops and boutiques, frequently letting themselves be lured in for a cup of coffee or tea. They almost always made a purchase or two and at the end of the outing, they would gather at The Tea Room to read Councilman Glen Boyd's poetry in the weekly newspaper. They also discussed social events or rumors while they moved strawberry-filled croissants and sweet rolls around on their plates with their forks. Almost every time they met, there was a new rumor; the storyteller declaring that she knew the source to be trustworthy. There was much discussion about the mayor, JoVonna, her child and what was supposed to be going on in each of their lives. No one knew for certain.

The Mississippi rains lulled the town to sleep that evening. The residents of Richland Hills were completely unaware of what was going to happen the next morning. Marcus stood in the mirror, clean-shaven and fussing with the tie that Lilly had selected. A small part of his conscience was in disagreement with what he was about to do, but when he thought about what he and Lilly had been through, he knew that he had to do this– to make a wrong right again. He pulled on the coat to his dark blue suit and straightened the tie that rested against his starched white shirt. Marcus picked up the phone, dialed Lilly's number and let it ring once, then hung up. It was a signal they shared that meant a combination of I Love You and I Am Leaving The House Now. Lilly looked over at the telephone and smiled as she thought to herself how wonderful it would be when she and Marcus were married. She continued to fasten her silk stockings to her garter belt. She had selected a black dress, which she thought was symbolic of what was to take place today. She envisioned the bitch that was JoVonna's soul being buried today, with her carcass left for all eyes of Richland Hills to ogle over.

Marcus parked his Cadillac in the space reserved for him in front of City Hall. It was customary for camera crews to use the parking spaces in the rear of the building and he was especially grateful for that on this day. The press had come because Marcus had dangled just enough in their faces to cause them to smell a story. As he walked along the path that led to the revolving doors, Marcus thought about the time he would spend celebrating with Lilly after his confrontation with JoVonna and involuntarily flashed pretty white teeth that formed a perfect smile. He greeted several people at the elevator. No one knew that there would be anything unusual about this meeting except Marcus and Lilly. Some of those present grumbled under their breath about the duration of the quarterly meetings, but there was at least one person standing there that would have come if

Marcus had called a meeting at two o'clock in the morning, in the rain, on the steps of the City Hall.

Lilly positioned herself at an angle in front of a window facing the front parking area. Marcus finished shaking hands and on cue, was speaking into the television cameras about cleaning up some of the issues that constituted "black eyes" for the city and how he planned to continue an honest and steadfast tenure as mayor. When JoVonna's Mercedes pulled up, Lilly nodded at Marcus and he casually glanced at his watch to note the six minutes that it should take JoVonna to get to the conference room. Lilly turned her head back to watch the arrogant and selfish young woman in the expensive navy blue, tailored suit and white blouse walk toward the building. She took solace in the fact that after today, if JoVonna wanted any respect in this town, she'd have to open her purse very wide to get it. Marcus cleared his throat and excused himself and left the room. Lilly started to show slides of the outline Marcus spoke about and his efforts to address and act upon the city's issues. The cameramen quickly became bored with the talk of landfills and proposals to renovate the library and wondered if they should wrap this story up, put away their equipment and leave it to the news desk to pull together the summary. The fact that so much happened in this town when you least expected it kept them filming. This meeting had gone on for just over ten minutes now and while the council members listened intently, the television crews had started to eye one another. Lilly apologized for Marcus' absence and said she was sure he would be right back. In the meantime, she kept everyone busy with all of the facts and figures she rapidly fired at them.

Marcus opened the door to his office just as JoVonna rounded the corner. She walked right up to him and tried to kiss him. He held her at arms length.

"What, no kiss for the mother of your child?'

"Let's step into my office and take a look at the papers you brought. JoVonna opened her briefcase and took out the folders containing what she claimed was her new documentation on the community within a community. Marcus took it all from her and locked it in his desk.

"What are you doing?" She protested.

"We will save that for later. Right now, I want you to come to the conference room and find out what we are doing to resolve some of the situations in this town. Be prepared to give a few remarks after I finish my statement."

JoVonna followed him without hesitation. When Marcus opened the door to his office, he looked to his left. Lilly opened the door to the conference room. She nodded, indicating that the conference call was in place. The room was silent as JoVonna entered, and when she saw the cameras, she cursed under her breath and wished she had checked her appearance and stopped for a drink. She straightened her jacket and moved her long hair from where it rested on her shoulder so that it cascaded down her back. Marcus took the podium, thanked Lilly for carrying on in his absence and began his statement.

"I've asked you all here today in an effort to make the entire city aware of my strategy for a good governing body. The first thing we need to do is take the lies and scandal out of politics. On that note, there is a matter I must clear up. I realize that some of you were out of town for the holiday. That is why I have waited until now to come forward with this statement." Marcus hesitated briefly to make sure he had everyone's undivided attention.

"I am definitely not the father of JoVonna Rossier's child." Eyebrows raised, mouths opened; one of the councilmen spilled a glass of water. Both cameras zoomed in for a close-up shot.

"I have here a document that I obtained from the Richland Hills hospital that clearly indicates that my blood type is A positive. JoVonna Rossier's blood type is also A positive, but the child's blood type is O. That means I could not possibly be that child's father." Marcus held up the document showing the results of the blood test and the cameras featured it. "Nurse Brenda Billford at Richland Hills hospital is on a conference call and will substantiate what I have said. She is also willing to repeat these facts in a court of law. I have enough copies for everyone. Lilly began passing out the copies of the report. As she got closer to JoVonna, she could almost feel the heat that was a byproduct of JoVonna's anger and surprise. Marcus spoke into the microphone.

"Perhaps Miss Rossier would like to make a comment at this time." The camera lenses whirred as they focused in on JoVonna. They stayed trained on her as she rose. She snatched a copy of the report from Lilly and stood with her eyes transfixed on the paper. Her mouth was dry. She was suddenly aware of the weight of her hair and she could feel perspiration trickle down her back. Thoughts swirled around in JoVonna's head.

I was so sure, she thought,...so sure. Marcus wanted me the night of the party. He wanted revenge after the banquet too....the newspapers said he was drunk that night........no one else had a motive..it HAD to have been him...

JoVonna's thoughts were now a blurred haze, but the nurse's voice on the telephone verifying what Marcus had just said jabbed at her like a poker turning coals in a hot fire. JoVonna was sure that after reading all the newspapers and asking as many questions as she did that she had figured out what happened the night of the banquet. So sure that it had never even crossed her mind to try to find out what Marcus' blood type was. The microphones were in JoVonna's face and Lilly and Marcus looked at each other, their eyes indicating to each other that their plan had succeeded. JoVonna was embarrassed and humiliated and worst of all, even her wit and sarcasm were no weapons against the shot of revenge that had just been fired at her. She knew two things: one, that she would not be reduced to tears and two, that no matter what it took, she was going to find out who had fathered her child, and when she did, the rest of his life belonged to her. He would have hell to pay.

"This is not nearly over yet!" She screamed into the microphone.

She left the room without further comment. As Marcus and the others packed up and prepared to go, the telephone lines in Marcus' office lit up, one after the other with messages that spanned a range from "It's about damned time!" to "We have always been behind you." Marcus and Lilly were satisfied. JoVonna was driving home, and there was so much unleashed anger within her that she could hardly breath. It seemed to her as though everyone she passed must have seen the broadcast and now she imagined that they jeered and pointed at her. In reality, some of them feared for their jobs, but still laughed at her in the privacy of their own homes. She reached into her glove compartment and pulled out the sterling silver flask. She drank all of the liquor in it, and was grateful for the fact that soon she would be home where she could fix another drink and she would be numb, at least for now.

All of the customers in the Blueridge Street Deli were still talking amongst themselves about what they had seen and heard the mayor say on television. Raphael and Glen Boyd sat at the counter and listened to the conversation two women were having at the table behind them.

"Who do you suppose really is the father?"

"I don't know. I wonder if she really did sleep with the mayor. Maybe there is something wrong with that blood test he was talking about. I heard he was the last one to leave that party she gave for him. Maybe they did something that night and he really did go back over there after the banquet."

JoVonna parked her car and got out as though she expected someone to step out from behind the trees and chide her about her illegitimate son. She cursed under her breath as she walked up the very steep incline and through

112

the old gate that swung open every time the wind blew. She entered through the doors that led in from her gardens. JoVonna stood at the kitchen counter and looked at the list Margot had prepared for the butcher.

"Add steak to this list and then go get it now!" Margot finished changing the baby and glanced out of the side of her eye to see JoVonna mixing a drink. She shook her head in silent disapproval and reached for the keys to the Cadillac. When Margot got to the door, JoVonna yelled out for her to take the baby with her. Margot did not want to do it, but decided that now was not a good time to confront JoVonna about the way that she failed to tend to Michael George the way any mother should. Besides, she thought, JoVonna must be going out of her mind after the mayor's statement. Margot lifted up the baby blanket and looked at the baby and smiled. After she had placed the baby in the car, she looked over at him again and cooed. "Well, now, just who *is* your daddy?" The child's toothless smile was especially funny to her at that moment, and she laughed out loud. She put her check and the deposit ticket for the bank on the seat beside her as she drove off the property. It was a much bigger deposit since JoVonna raised her salary by 10 percent the day after their fight. The scars from the fork were almost invisible, but Margot had not forgotten what happened on that day.

JoVonna sat in her library drinking and thinking. She picked up the telephone and asked for the date of the next council meeting from the voice on the other end. She was given the date and marked her calendar accordingly. JoVonna was still angry and felt as though she had been on the losing side of not a fight, but a full-scale war with Marcus and Lilly. It was time to fight back. She lay across her bed to formulate a plan that would net her the information she needed. When she was finished, she went about her normal routine of watching the families, and even how many visitors they had now, writing down everything they did and her justification for why, in her eyes, whatever they did was wrong.

Marcus followed Lilly to her house and as they walked up the steps to the front porch, she chided him about redecorating his office. He agreed with a simple nod of his head. Once inside, their attention was focused on what happened earlier that morning. Marcus thought about what they had done to JoVonna and smiled.

"What do you suppose JoVonna is doing right now?" Marcus asked as he poured champagne in two glasses.

Lilly sat thinking a moment. "I couldn't begin to guess. If what she said when she held her press conference is true, and someone really did drug her, who do you suppose it was?"

"I don't know, but somebody in this town has got a real problem with her or something she did, and that could be any number of people."

Marcus saw the devilish smirk on Lilly's face.

"What?"

"Who do you think she was sleeping with? Do you think she knows who the father is, or do you believe someone else really did what she said? Do you think she was pregnant before that night and used your name to try to cover up her mistake?

"I don't know, and I don't care." Marcus said.

"What do you think the council members thought about what happened today?"

"That's a good question, Lilly. Some of them seemed amused; others seemed to be confused."

Marcus thought back to the day he had asked the council members for help in winning the election. He thought about the lengthy meeting they had after he left the room. He also knew of a couple of times they met informally after that. He discarded the thoughts and focused on the fact that Lilly was toying with the buckle on his belt.

Marcus turned around to face her and they toasted the success of their plan.

"Lilly."

"Yes?"

He helped her step out of her skirt.

"I love you."

She took his drink and put it down on the table.

"I love you too."

She folded his pants across the chair next to her bed. Marcus unfastened her brassiere and kissed her breasts. He kneeled down and took off her panties. Lilly closed her eyes and they celebrated well into the evening.

JoVonna waited impatiently for the day of the council meeting and now she paced the floors of her mansion like a caged animal, watching the clock. At the appropriate time, she picked up the briefcase that she had filled with money and threw the Mohair jacket that matched her skirt over her shoulders. She wanted answers, and she was prepared to buy them from whoever was willing to sell. JoVonna's Mercedes purred as she turned the key and headed for the meeting the mayor and council members were having at City Hall. She took the parking space reserved for Glen Boyd and pulled the briefcase from the passenger side of the car. Glen rounded the corner, saw JoVonna in his parking spot and was forced to take a visitor space. He threw down his cigar stub and deliberately quickened his step until he was in front of her. She watched him walk up the stairs ahead of her.

A two-hundred-pound, bald headed, slew-footed, gap-toothed man who writes poetry for the town newspaper. What a pitiful excuse of a man, she thought. She shook her head from side to side in disgust and pursed her lips.

JoVonna walked up the stairs and stopped to use the pay phone near council's chamber. When Marcus' secretary answered, JoVonna spoke quickly, pretending to cry so as to disguise her voice.

"Mayor Brackner's office, this is Donna."

"Donna, tell him it is Lilly. I have an emergency and I need to speak with him right away." JoVonna sniffed again and when Donna put her on hold to go and get Marcus, JoVonna hung up. She watched, hiding behind one of the large columns in the hallway as Donna entered the council chamber. A moment later, Marcus moved quickly through the door. JoVonna smiled when she saw the concern etched in his face as he headed back to his office. Donna followed. JoVonna waited until they were out of sight and then walked through the door of the council chamber.

All heads turned. Bob Givens looked at her from head to toe with a sneer, then took out his handkerchief and spat into it. Henry Talbert and Billy Ray Thompson stared out of lust. Leroy Wilkins wondered if his brother would ever find another job. His brother had worked at one of JoVonna's stores until he insisted on a raise. He had been accused of stealing several boxes of merchandise and fired the next day. Some of the council members waited anxiously for what was about to happen, and still others just waited. She walked over to the table, opened the briefcase full of money and began to speak to her attentive audience.

"All of you were in attendance on the evening of the mayor's banquet. That means that there is a good possibility that someone in this room has the answers to my questions. If you have the answers I want, then the cash is yours." She closed up the briefcase filled with $150,000 in one-hundred-dollar bills and quickly walked out of the room. Her fragrance loomed on, reminding them of her presence moments earlier. Some commented. Others just listened, saying nothing. When Marcus returned, muttering something about Lilly being fine and a wild goose chase, they filled him in on what had just happened.

Margot had established a friendship with Bill Henderson, the owner of the butcher shop, and as he filled her order, he joked about JoVonna being his most particular customer. "I save all of the order forms you bring in for JoVonna for at least one full year, just in case.

"Really?"

"Yeah, really." he replied.

She smiled and took her packages containing various cuts of fresh meat and left.

Two days passed, each having almost identical agendas. JoVonna went to the office; Shirley took aspirin. After work, JoVonna was seated comfortably in her library at home. She watched her neighbors and made notes to add to the proposal she was writing in another obsessive effort to discourage them from living there. Some of them were getting new roofs and she wrote in her notes that the quality of the materials should be inspected as well as the fact that someone needed to check to see if they had obtained proper city permits for whatever that drab little building was they were constructing at the edge of their property.

JoVonna's thoughts were constantly interrupted by her mind's on-going efforts to remember the night of the banquet. She kept having flashbacks. She could vaguely remember the fight with Lilly, the drive home, and fixing one last drink when she got home but after that, nothing. She had hired and fired a private investigator within a matter of days because they disagreed on strategy. Frustration motivated her now, and she examined the list Margot had made of everyone who attended the banquet that evening. She knew that the right amount of cash would make anybody whisper what he or she knew. JoVonna questioned key people who worked for her and was trying to think of a way to, as the investigator had put it, 'flush out more sources'. Later that day, she listened to the telephone ring twice, and realizing that Margot had opted to try to quiet the baby rather than answer it, JoVonna picked it up.

"Uhhh. Miss Rossier? A handkerchief muffled the voice.

"Yes"

"I have some information for you. Even more than you asked for, but it's going to cost you twice what you were willing to pay earlier," the voice said.

"Who is this?" JoVonna listened attentively to see if there was anything familiar about the voice.

"My name is not a part of the deal. Are you buying?"

"Fine." JoVonna stood, and upset the drink on the table next to her. She was angry about having to pay twice what she had previously offered.

"If it is going to cost me $300,000 now, I want a sample of what I am buying, or no deal."

"Okay. I know that Marcus is planning on buying some very expensive jewelry that Lilly has been admiring at a store just outside of town."

"I don't want his damned shopping list," she hissed.

"Okay, okay." The voice sounded panicky now. "Marcus is looking for a partner to assume 51% of a joint venture. He's putting a lot of cash into the deal– I know details."

"What else?" she said between sips.

"He is looking to lease another building so Lilly can expand her business."

"Enough of that. What do you know about the night of the banquet and the father of this child?"

The voice was still muffled, but louder now.

"I accidentally overhead a telephone conversation the night of the banquet. I know what happened to you that night. I mean, I know everything." He nursed a bottle of beer while he decided how much more to disclose to her over the telephone. "I have already given you a lot of information that you can use. I have a lot more details if you are serious about finding out who is messing with you. Just be a little creative and you can make some things happen to help yourself. From this point on, it's a cash-first deal."

"Okay." she said. "When and how?"

"There is an old abandoned bank just outside of town. Do you know where it is?"

"Yes, I know where it is. When?"

"Can you have all the cash by Friday?"

"That won't be a problem."

"Okay, Friday then, at the bank at six o'clock. Bring your deposit and you can withdraw as much information as you need." He laughed and hung up. He never even noticed the shadow of the two feet outside his door.

JoVonna spent the days until her meeting at the bank using the information she received. First she tied a headscarf around her neck and put on several layers of clothing under a light coat to appear heavier. She put on much more makeup than was usual and donned sunglasses. She took off all her jewelry, left her Mercedes at a restaurant and took a taxi to where the voice on the phone said the jewelry store was located just outside of town. In a nasal twang, she told the cab driver that she was feeling ill and asked if he would take a package inside for her. She sat in the taxi watching as the cab driver handed over the package to the owner. It contained enough cash to buy the sapphire and diamond necklace as well as the loose stones that the jeweler had been holding for Marcus. The taxi driver also handed him a note with delivery instructions that contained what appeared to be Marcus' signature.

Two days later, Marcus surprised Lilly and told her that he had the jeweler put aside the pieces of jewelry she admired earlier. When they went to purchase the pieces that Marcus had reserved, they were informed that the jewelry had already been paid for and delivered. Marcus expressed concern and denied having signed anything. The jeweler pulled the card that contained the instructions. It was typewritten and said: Deliver to 21834 Mountain Crest Road. Have the card read: I Still Love You, signed Marcus. The jeweler remembered that a man had paid for the jewelry and that he appeared to have a fare in the car but she did not match the description that Marcus gave the jeweler of JoVonna. Still, the delivery address was JoVonna's. Marcus and Lilly figured that JoVonna had something to do with it, but they could not figure out how she would have known about the jewelry. Lilly intended to wear the missing pieces of jewelry on her wedding day, and she was hurt. One angry tear slid down her cheek. She was certain of one thing, and that was that she was not going to let that bitch drive another wedge between Marcus and herself. This time she would believe her man.

JoVonna stayed one step ahead of them. The next morning, she went to the site of the building that Marcus was about to sign a lease agreement on so that Lilly could expand her printing business. She spent the remainder of morning and part of the afternoon negotiating with the owner to buy the building. She gave him a hefty bonus to act as a liaison until after Marcus signed the contract to lease it. She stipulated in her contract with the former owner that she would pay the total price he asked for the building in cash, but only after it was occupied. She would let Lilly move in, then toy with her.

She sat in her car and laughed on the way back to the mansion. The high heels she wore made the steep path leading from her garages to the back of the mansion burdensome. Once inside, she made a drink and changed into a French-vanilla silk robe. While she drank, she looked over the organization charts of her companies for names of anyone she thought might have information pertaining to her search for the father of her child. These people would be questioned, some for the second time. If she suspected they knew something but would not tell her, they would be fired.

JoVonna was about to lose her mind going over newspapers again, questioning people, interrogating Margot and even speaking with the police chief to see if anyone might have any clues. She threw a stack of newspaper articles on the floor and pinned her hair up. The paper she was reading had become a blur and still, she continued to stare at it. Determination nurtured a new inner strength in her and she had sworn to herself and said more than once to Margot that she would not stop until she found out who it was that had so drastically changed her life.

She refreshed her drink and began to make plans as to how she would continue to monitor Marcus' joint venture. When it was finalized, she would pay whatever was necessary to gain a controlling interest. She snapped her notebook closed and tried to sleep while mentally scrolling through her agenda for the next morning.

JoVonna spent Friday morning at her office in Waltham Towers. The minutes ticked away slowly on the Wittnauer watch she wore and she wished that she had made the appointment with her newly established informant for earlier in the day. She wanted to go and get that information now! Instead, she had two very lengthy meetings scheduled. She was no longer as uncomfortable with the probing eyes and assuming looks that had resulted from Marcus' press conference. She told the board members to go to hell in the first few minutes of the 9:00 a.m. meeting and was now back in the saddle and ready to ride right on to the next meeting that was about to convene in her conference room. That was on the outside, anyway. On the inside, the liquor she had for breakfast had worked its way through her system. Her nerves were starting to frazzle because it seemed to her that time was standing still. Her mind told her that it would never be six o'clock and she would never know who was responsible for drugging and impregnating her.

She nibbled at the catered lunch and went back to her office. JoVonna looked at the picture of her parents on her desk and wished again that they could be there; that all of the horrendous things that had happened were just some sort of nightmare that she was trapped in. She left for the evening, drove home and waited for Margot. When Margot walked through the door, both women were immediately angry. JoVonna was angry because Margot had taken so long and Margot was angry because JoVonna couldn't even wait until she put the baby down before she started in with what had to be done.

"Your baby had a doctor's appointment today. Didn't you know that?" Margot glared at her boss.

JoVonna mumbled something about her calendar being at the office and went to her bedroom. Every time she looked at that child now, it reminded her that a segment of her life had been blocked out. The fact that there were so many missing pieces from that time angered her again as she dressed for her six o'clock appointment. She seldom wore slacks; her legs were one of her assets and she knew it. This evening though, she opted for a simple dark pantsuit with flat black leather shoes and basic jewelry. The bank had been vacant for a long time now, and she turned up her nose at the thought of how dusty it would be. She pulled both of the cases full of money from underneath her bed and checked them once again. One last drink, and she would be on her way. She walked back down the steep path to her Mercedes. Looking to her right, she could see the steeple of the church that her neighbors had built and was once again reminded of her ongoing battle. She recalled a spirited conversation she had with Marcus when he suggested one time that she just build another home someplace else on the land she owned. She was angry then, and she was angry now, just thinking about his stupid suggestion. She would work on her new plans for getting rid of her neighbors at the bottom of the hill in more detail later. Right now, she was about to find out who the father of her child was, why she had been drugged and who was behind all of it.

As she was driving, JoVonna thought about what she would do in retaliation to the person or persons who had brought so much turmoil into her life and her home. She would not involve the police. They had been useless in their investigation when she called them after Marcus' little setup proved that he was not the father of her child and that someone else had been responsible for the debacle on the night of the banquet. She could still recall the officer's words:

"Ms. Rossier, there is simply nothing here. There are no footprints, no fingerprints, no broken glass, no sign of forced entry into your safe that would account for the large sum of money and confidential documents you are reporting missing, no evidence – nothing. Of course we'll let you know the moment we get a lead on this, but it happened so long ago. It must have rained ten or fifteen times since then." She remembered him standing there, shaking his head and comparing his notes to those of one of the other officers. He put the notebook in his pocket and returned to one of three squad cars that drove through the wrought iron security gate and exited her property.

She dismissed the thought and drove on, her body rigid with anticipation. She would handle this herself. JoVonna made the last turn off the main road and followed a path formed with smooth white pebbles. She pulled up and stopped abruptly. There was one other car parked on the side of the boarded up building. The color, make and model were a blur to her as she focused her undivided attention on pulling out the cases of money to go and buy the information she wanted. It was dark inside, and a cool dampness loomed inside the building. JoVonna was forced to stop just inside to allow herself to adjust to the blackness and the horrible stench. She struck the matches she found in her purse. She made her way past the tellers' cages that were laced with cobwebs and on around past the large vault door that looked as if it were about to fall off its hinges. The darkness irritated her. Finally she came to an area where two very large windows had been boarded up. A single stream of daylight shined through the crack and provided all the light she needed to see the man across the room sitting in a chair with his back to her. A coal oil lamp sat on the floor beside him. JoVonna quickly became indignant about the fact that this man, her informant, must have known she was standing there, yet he kept his back to her.

"Look, whoever you are, I am paying for this time, and I don't intend to wait another minute!"

She walked around to the front of the chair. When she saw his face, she breathed in but could not make herself exhale. JoVonna recognized Henry Talbert as a City Council member, but only by looking at his eyes. What used to be his mouth and the entire lower half of his face had been blown away with what must have been a large caliber gun. The fingers on his right hand had been cut off and jagged pieces of skin barely covered the stubs. Pinned to his chest was a note written in bold letters that read "No News Today." She read the note and felt faint. There was a salty taste in her mouth. JoVonna's hands still clutched the two bags of money that now felt weightless because of her adrenaline. She stared at the disfigured face, still unable to turn away. She was afraid and wanted to cry, but no sound would come. Screams exploded in her head, but still, none were audible. When she could make her feet move, she quickly followed the streaks of daylight back out of the bank and threw the bags in her car. Before she could get into the car, she became violently ill. When her stomach was empty, she took a flask of liquor from her glove compartment and rinsed her mouth out and spat. Then she drained the remainder of the contents while she drove home. Her thoughts were a series of questions....*Who killed Henry? ....Why?...How did they know what he was going to tell her?.....Was it over now?...Did they think she already knew something? And, most importantly, what did they, whoever they were, intend to do about it?*

For the next two days, she watched the news and drank. Henry Talbert's body had not yet been discovered. She gazed at the patterns the rain was making on her windows and thought about what she must do next to solve the mysteries in her life. She finally took the money out of the bags that she had jammed under her bed two days earlier and returned it to her safe. On the third day after she had found Henry dead, there was a newspaper article reporting the discovery of Henry Talbert's body in the abandoned bank. Her heart rate increased and she panicked. The paper said that this case was unusual and would be extremely difficult to solve because of the number of fingerprints in the abandoned bank and the lack of other evidence found. The fingerprints were everywhere and they ranged from former employees and customers to young people who sneaked in the bank to make out. JoVonna mentally retraced her steps and was sure she had not touched anything on the way into the bank because she sat the bags down only long enough to strike a match. She pictured herself in the bank again, moving forward, past the tellers' cages and the vault. She felt sure that she had not put her hands on anything once she was inside because she remembered having the two bags in her hands all the time. Besides, when that bank was open for business, she had as much money in there as could be federally insured, which meant she made fairly regular visits. She sighed and began to relax a bit. She turned her thoughts to what she would do now, knowing that she would have to let this incident pass before she tried anything again. She did not want to be associated with Henry's death in any way.

She would have to concentrate on protecting herself. Now that she knew Marcus was innocent, she was afraid that whoever killed Henry might think Henry had already given her some news about who drugged and raped her. If the killer thought she could identify him, then it was only a matter of time before whoever it was would be trying to get to her to prevent her from seeking revenge or going to the police. She remembered a notice she had seen in a flyer earlier and thumbed through several papers in her library to see if she had kept it. She picked it up with one hand while writing a note with the other to remind Margot to get the filing done. In the flyer, a breeder advertised two Brindle Pit Bulls for sale: One male, one female. When JoVonna called him, he explained that the animals were fighters, each having been to the pit several times and holding their own.

"You are going to have to spend a hell of a lot of time getting to know these animals. I have been breeding one of my sets of parents this year and now I am going to keep the puppies and sell you the parents, that is if you are still interested."

JoVonna found herself biting her nails more often to keep from systematically reaching for a drink. She moved her hand with its gnawed nails away from her mouth and looked at it in disgust. Just the picture of the dogs scared her, but then, she told herself, that was the point.

"The deal also includes a galvanized steel cage large enough for the pair with a pull-up door and a runner."

She purchased the animals and their accessories over the phone.

"Now, your name again is…?"

"Carey. Robert Carey."

"Alright, Mr. Carey, my address is 21834 Mountain Crest Road."

JoVonna wrote her check for the amount he quoted and put it in the pocket of her skirt.

When he arrived later, she took meticulous notes while he instructed her on how to care for the animals. She could see the animals in his truck and her heart raced.

"Now be sure and give them some fresh, raw, ground-up chicken necks occasionally. It is good for their muscle tone."

JoVonna frowned. She wanted to tell the man to take his ugly dogs and leave, but fear of what might happen if she did not do something to protect herself moved her forward.

"Now, look, Uhhh……..Ms. Rossier, by its very nature, a Pit Bull will go after blood on anything, so don't cut yourself out there on that cage. Don't even knick yourself shaving your legs and then go near them." His face turned red as soon as he realized that what he said might have embarrassed her. Robert Carey took the check and set up the cage and runner. He brought the dogs around on leases, put them in the cage and left after cautioning her again about how powerful the dogs were. JoVonna stared at them from a distance. They were almost three years old and their chest span seemed to be as broad as that of a small man. She would work with Robert Carey until she felt comfortable putting the dogs on the runner that allowed them to get close enough to her back door to protect her property. She would also become more familiar with the necessities for taking care of them. She would have to interact with the animals to the extent that they would learn to protect only her. Robert had admonished her not to show fear and she wondered if the dogs knew what the scowl on her face meant.

After Mr. Carey left, JoVonna stood looking at the evidence of spring in her gardens. The dogs that Mr. Carey had just left offered a strange contrast to the beauty of the gardens with their colorful blooms, but JoVonna already felt safer. She had security gates in the front, but the fence in the back that had been constructed along the perimeter of her property had been put in place only as a noticeable separation between her land and that of her neighbors. The dogs would soon be trained to protect the area in and around the concrete wall that bordered two sides of her mansion. The other side, which was open and led down a very steep hill to her garages, was well lit. If someone should come up that path to her gardens, then the dogs could keep them away from the rear entrance to her mansion. She had pondered the thought of a gun, but after seeing what happened to Henry, that thought terrified her as much as the unknown person she was trying to protect herself from.

Margot had just returned from taking Michael George for his immunizations. When she came through the gate, the pit bulls barked and instinctually lunged at the pull-down door on the cage. The lock bounced back and forth against the cage door. JoVonna met them at the door, but did not take the child even though Margot was visibly shaken.

"What the hell is going on?" Margot shouted.

"I've purchased those dogs to protect us. I am worried about the fact that someone was in my home and drugged and raped me and I still don't know who it was. I've exhausted nearly all avenues of information, and the police don't know anything. I don't want guns in my home, so this was a good alternative. I will be the one primarily interacting with the animals. I will put them on their runners at night and feed them because I want them loyal only to me."

Margot loved dogs, but she sighed with relief at the news that she would not have this added responsibility and went to put the baby down for his nap. JoVonna spent the rest of her day in her library dictating letters for Shirley and reading up on the care and training of her animals. Later, she wrote a check to Raphael to begin making her summer clothes and made out the check for Margot's salary.

Margot stood in the sunlit kitchen nibbling on a piece of strawberry shortcake while she made out the list for the butcher. She daydreamed about what it would be like to be truly independent and happy. Right now, she took care of all of the needs of a child that was not even related to her. JoVonna condemned her wardrobe, her sex life and just about everything else about her. She was stuck here, and the older she got, the more time JoVonna had to use her up. She had saved her money and invested in the past, but she was not nearly as wealthy as she intended to be when she left this mansion. Every time she decided that she was fed up and that it was time to move on, she was reminded of the little boy that JoVonna had helped her bury. Every time she packed her bags, JoVonna reminded her of that night, but then always quickly followed up their arguments with more cash or another large gift. Margot was determined that she would never work for anyone again when she left here and she needed a whole lot of cash for that commitment, so she stayed on, slowing carrying out her plan.

THE RAIN WILL TELL
Chapter Twenty-Three

It was a warm, lazy Sunday afternoon and the sun winked at Richland Hills from behind occasional clouds. Magnolia and Lilac scented the air. Marcus and Lilly walked hand in hand in the park that was just a few blocks from his house.

"Are you nervous about the wedding?" Lilly asked.

"Not yet. What about you?"

"No, but we do still need to work out a backup plan with Glen in case the weather is inclement. It was so gracious of Glen to offer us his beautiful new home and gardens for the wedding."

"Yes, he's pretty proud of that house, and his family deserves it after having to wait all this time, living in that small duplex."

Marcus smoothed Lilly's hair back so he could see her face.

She picked up a dandelion and blew its fuzz in his face. He picked her up and carried her a short distance, then gently laid her down in the willowy grass. A family of birds nesting in a tree nearby serenaded them. Marcus rested on one elbow and looked at Lilly while they discussed JoVonna and her dilemma and all the unanswered questions surrounding her life. They also discussed Henry Talbert's death, and the fact that the police still had not been able to find the killer. Lilly had taken this whole ordeal on as a mystery that she wanted to solve. Their discussion soon stimulated their appetites and they left, heading back to Marcus' for a late lunch.

Across town, JoVonna sat in her library engrossed in her usual vigil. She watched as Willie Mae and Bessie and Bessie's husband, Whistler and the rest of that despicable little group of families set about the task of maintaining their gardens. She trained her binoculars on Whistler as he loaded the back of a beat-up station wagon with vegetables and drove off to sell them by the main highway. Some of the girls were big enough to help out in the community gardens now, and she watched them at work, with calico dresses and black and white oxford shoes. Their hair was always braided, thick, lumpy extensions from their heads suspended in mid air. She made more notes about checking plumbing codes on the proposal she wrote and finished her drink. She decided not to have a second drink but the sound of her son crying in the kitchen was incessant and it penetrated her nerves like needles. The fact that Margot had total responsibility for the child was another tension builder between the two women. Margot did not necessarily want the responsibility, but could not stand by while JoVonna failed at even the most basic attempts to give the child proper care. Margot was in the kitchen finishing cooking JoVonna's dinner and trying to complete a list for the butcher.

Michael George was restless and wanted to be picked up. He was getting bigger now and Margot could not maneuver around with him in her arms as easily as she used to. The child continued to cry and JoVonna got up and went to see why Margot had not quieted him.

"Why is my son still crying?"

"I would guess that he would like a little attention from his mother." Margot said, with her hand on her hip.

"What are you implying?" JoVonna raised both eyebrows.

The two women argued; Margot reminded JoVonna that the child was hers as she headed out the door for her own dinner plans. About thirty minutes later JoVonna pinned her hair up and decided to take the restless child for a drive. She thought that maybe the drive would make Michael stop crying and go to sleep. As she drove along, gazing at the pre-summer stage that nature was setting, she decided to go into town. She turned onto Culver Street where the flowers were abundant and the trees formed a green arch. She recognized the Cadillac immediately, but wondered why Margot would be parked outside of the town's most expensive restaurant. She went around the block and parked. Michael George had fallen asleep. JoVonna wished she had remembered to fill her liquor flask. She was tempted to go in and order a drink; instead, she tapped her manicured nails lightly against her steering wheel and waited.

A few minutes later, Margot left the restaurant with Timothy Wells, the vice president of Rossier Industries. JoVonna could not imagine why the vice president of her company would be having dinner with Margot, but it made her suspicious and angry. She wondered what an officer at her company could possibly have to do with Margot. She followed them until they turned off to a hotel. JoVonna wished she had time to go and get a camera and take pictures to send to the bastard's wife, but she had a much more important task at hand. She peeled away, causing a cloud of dust to form behind her. When she got back to the mansion, she put the sleeping baby in his bed and ran to Margot's quarters. She searched under the bed, in all the drawers, in the flower vase and under the rugs but found nothing. She would have to search the Cadillac later. She glanced at the cat sitting on Margot's window ledge.

JoVonna heard thunder and stepped forward to close the window. As she stepped back, her arm brushed against the drapes, causing a crackling sound. She thought that was odd and looked to see what had caused the noise. There, pinned to the inside of the thick drapes were several confidential documents pertaining to JoVonna's holdings. She was amazed at how many stock certificates Margot owned, both for Rossier Industries and other companies. There were copies of minutes from her board meetings with little symbols added in the margins. There were copies of confidential memos, and taped to the bottom of the drapes was a key. When JoVonna stooped to look more closely, she recognized it as a key to her office. There was a metal box on the floor with a key taped to the bottom. When JoVonna opened it, she was aghast at how much cash was inside. She didn't quite know what Margot had planned, but she was furious. Her first instinct was to tear all of this down and fire Margot, but she didn't know how much information Margot had already used or sold, nor did she know how much Margot had committed to memory and that worried her tremendously. She left everything in place and even opened the window back up a couple of inches just like Margot had left it. Then she went to her bedroom to drink and think. She dialed the home phone number for Timothy Wells, her vice president at Rossier Industries. When his wife answered, JoVonna spoke through a handkerchief and told his wife what hotel he was at and that he was with a woman. She went on to describe his car and what Margot was wearing. When she had finished convincing his wife to go and see for herself, she hung up.

THE RAIN WILL TELL
Chapter Twenty-Four

Summer was beautiful. The trees stood full and majestic, bearing their fruits. The roses were a symphony of fragrances; the grass was a plush green carpet. JoVonna lingered in the sun each morning when she went out to feed the mammoth animals. They were loyal to no one but her now. She had to hire a new lawn service. The men that had maintained her lawn and trees previously now refused to go in her back yard, even with the animals in their cage. JoVonna smirked as she handed the men their last check and made a point to stand right next to the cage, almost daring them to come close enough to get their money. The dogs rocked the cage violently until the men left. Days passed and JoVonna was ambivalent about what she had recently started doing to the dogs, but for the fourth day in a row, she poured perfume around the edges of their food bowl. She kept them in their cage now and pushed the contaminated food in with a rod, using a small feeding slot instead of opening the door. She made a mental note to throw the food bowl away and replace it with a new one on Thursday after she taunted the dogs for the last time. The dogs howled and looked at her now with hungry and evil eyes.

JoVonna and Margot had not seen much of each other since Margot came home early Monday morning, after JoVonna spotted her leaving the restaurant the evening before. Margot had prepared herself for JoVonna's lecture about staying out all night but JoVonna didn't say a word. She did not want Margot or Timothy to know that she knew anything until she found out how their scheme against her was supposed to unfold. It was obvious that Timothy's wife had not gotten there before they left the hotel. She was a big, plain woman who was always afraid someone was going to take Timothy from her and she would certainly have hurt Margot if she had seen her with her husband at that hotel.

JoVonna decided that now she would have to call Timothy's house and pretend to be the other woman. She knew enough about Timothy or Tim, as she would refer to him when she spoke to his wife, to convince his wife that he was sleeping around. She intended to break his marriage up because he was obviously helping Margot with her plans, whatever they were. JoVonna knew now that Margot was still buying as much stock as possible in her holdings. She frequently checked behind the curtains and in the small metal box hidden in Margot's room for evidence of new wealth. She also knew from documents she found that Margot had purchased at least two properties in town and that she had been looking at homes for sale. JoVonna still did not know exactly what Margot was planning, but she firmly believed that with all of the evidence she had found, and the secret they shared that could send them both to jail, that Margot had something to do with her being drugged and raped on the night of the banquet, and for that, Margot would pay dearly.

The two women came face to face in the kitchen. Margot fed the baby; JoVonna ate her breakfast and read over some reports. Neither of the women spoke, but both had full mental agendas. JoVonna watched her like a cat preying on a fattened mouse, as Margot stood rigid, with her back turned. She wanted to get out now, but her need for more monetary security convinced her to stay. Margot worried about what would happen to the child when she left and pondered whether she should just take him with her. She could put her properties up for sale and leave Mississippi with the baby, but she had to consider what kind of legal ramifications she would have to contend with. JoVonna's attorneys were barracudas. She also had to consider the restraints a young child would impose her plans to return to school, pursue modeling again and travel. With our without the child, she knew she would be leaving soon. That evening, JoVonna made the first of several calls to Timothy Well's house.

"Hello?"

"Hello, Mrs. Wells. I spent the night in a hotel with your husband Sunday."

"Who the hell is this?"

"I am the woman who is going to take Tim away from you. You know, I love it when he calls my name and kisses me and tells me he is leaving you for me."

Timothy's wife slammed down the phone and fumed. JoVonna spent the next four days planning for Margot's birthday and when Margot came home from the butcher shop that Friday evening, JoVonna was waiting to surprise her. It was a rare occasion because JoVonna had been drinking, but in order for her plan to be successful, she actually had to pretend that she was more intoxicated than she really was. She stood in the kitchen wearing a white apron that had been heavily stained with chicken blood from preparing the ground up meat for her dogs.

Margot frowned like she did every time JoVonna prepared the chicken for the dogs. JoVonna fixed a smile on her face and wished Margot happy birthday. She gestured towards the gift on the counter. Margot opened it and gasped. It was a beautiful blue, sequined dress. She immediately felt less apprehensive than she had the previous two weeks and appreciated the fact that JoVonna was using her birthday to relieve some of the tension in the mansion. She took it out of the box and noticed Raphael's signature on the tag. JoVonna handed Margot a glass of champagne and told her to go try the dress on. Margot thanked her and went to change into the dress. When she came back, JoVonna handed her another drink and complimented her on how beautiful she looked in the dress. The two women continued to talk about general town gossip while JoVonna topped off Margot's drink every time she turned her back. When Margot started to slur and suggested that maybe she ought to go to bed, JoVonna protested. "No, it's your birthday and I made reservations at the finest restaurant in town. Just keep your dress on. I'll go put my dress on and we can go and celebrate." JoVonna said casually, "Oh, I have something

135

else for you." She reached under the counter for the antique atomizer filled with perfume. JoVonna had unscrewed the top earlier, and in a drunken performance, pretended at first that she did not notice the perfume seeping out. She turned the bottle back upright and told Margot that what was left was for her. Both women laughed. JoVonna wiped the perfume from her hands onto the apron and then took the apron off and cleaned up the remainder of the perfume with it. She walked away from the counter and then turned and said, "Oh hell!"

"What's the matter?" Margot said very slowly. She reeled backwards and then held on to a chair for support. JoVonna knew she was drunk.

"I forgot to feed the dogs. It's your birthday and I decided to fix a special meal for them to celebrate too. Will you slip that apron on over your dress and take that chicken out to them?" Margot looked at the tray of raw, bloody meat. JoVonna had decorated the tray with garnish and vegetables and Margot laughed at the thought of the dogs celebrating her birthday.

Margot hesitated. "You know I don't like to go near that cage. Those dogs bark at me. I don't think they like me." She sat the tray back down on the counter.

JoVonna laughed. "It is the dogs' nature to bark. Besides, they will love you tonight when they see the fine meal you are bringing them. Go ahead. Just put the tray in the cage and then we can go celebrate. You will have to unlock the door instead of using the feeding slot because this tray is too large to fit into the feeding slot. You just wait and see. They will love to see you coming with their special dinner. They may even eat the parsley too." Both women laughed. She picked the tray up and handed it back to Margot.

JoVonna waited a minute and then looked out the kitchen window to watch her plan in motion. The dogs reacted immediately to the perfume that Margot had been given as a birthday present. They recognized the perfume that had prevented them from eating the food that sat right in front of them for the past few days. They stood like soldiers, ready to seek revenge. Margot had barely opened the door when the dogs attacked the fragrance that had penetrated and tormented their keen sense of smell and poisoned their food for several days. They lunged at the tray of food and the apron Margot wore that was stained with the chicken blood that would now provide the nourishment they had been deprived of. Margot only screamed once before the more powerful of the two dogs leaped forward and locked onto her throat with his mighty jaws. The other dog tore away at her abdomen, ripping the apron and her flesh to shreds. Margot's body convulsed as the dogs dragged her by her hair and gnawed and chewed her extremities. She lay flat on her back, her hands ineffectually pushing at the mammoth animals.

JoVonna was shaken and affected by what she saw and had to turn away from the window. She vomited in her sink and turned on the water to wash it away. The truth came suddenly. JoVonna had actually arranged for her dogs to kill Margot. The dogs circled Margot, as if they dared her to show a sign of life. They had carried out their master's plan, and now the scent of evil commingled with the blood and perfume. JoVonna drank straight from the bottle now. She made herself look again a few minutes later. Margot had stopped moving and JoVonna felt sure that she was dead. JoVonna made three calls: the police, animal control and an ambulance. She sat down and had another drink. When the police came, JoVonna went through her rehearsed story. It was Margot's birthday, she explained, and they were going out to celebrate. Since their reservations were at 8 o'clock, they needed to hurry. Margot had gotten dressed first. JoVonna went on to explain to the officers that Margot thought it would be hilarious if the dogs celebrated her birthday too. They both had laughed at the thought and Margot had slipped the apron on over her new dress to take the dogs their birthday dinner. JoVonna explained that after a few minutes she heard what sounded like a scream. When she went to the door, Margot was lying still. The dogs were standing over her.

"Is there a next of kin?" one of the officers inquired.

"Not to my knowledge. Margot responded to a newspaper advertisement. She was a very private person. I know that her parents are deceased and that she was an only child. She never mentioned any other relatives."

"Do you have any idea why the dogs attacked her?"

"None at all. I put the dogs on a runner in the gardens every night. Sometimes Margot came in late but the dogs never bothered her. Margot loved animals and we decided to get the dogs to protect all of us after I was drugged and raped in my own home.

"I am sorry about that ma'am."

"I've got to speak with the Coroner." The officer flipped to a new page in his notebook and walked away.

JoVonna's gardens were full of people now. Animal Control tranquilized and fitted the dogs with muzzles and led them away.

Several of the police officers talked to their sergeant. Others roped off the area while pictures were taken and evidence was gathered. The media swarmed, vying for the opportunity to take the best pictures. The Coroner covered Margot's body and shook his head, wishing he had not eaten such a big dinner.

When the flurry of activity was over, JoVonna was given a number to call if she thought of any additional information. She walked back into her kitchen from the stagnant night air and sat down and began to massage her temples. JoVonna noticed that her hands were trembling and wondered if the officers had noted that in the large notebooks they filled up with details surrounding Margot's death. Her thoughts shifted. By killing Margot and destroying all of the documents she found, JoVonna felt she had put an end to all the things Margot had planned against her. In her efforts to destroy the man she believed had helped Margot, JoVonna had continued to call Timothy's house. JoVonna knew that sooner or later his wife would get angry enough to do something about the phone calls she kept getting. JoVonna would seek her satisfaction in the vengeance Timothy's wife would eventually inflict upon him.

She had solved one problem, but when the baby started to cry, she was reminded that she had created another one. She picked the child up awkwardly and heated his bottle in a pot filled with hot water as she had seen Margot do. She had only changed the baby's diaper a few times before and it proved to be a task. When she finally got the child quiet and back in the bed, she knew that she would have to advertise for someone to replace Margot as soon as possible. Once again the town of Richland Hills would be passing time talking about what happened high atop the hill at JoVonna's mansion.

JoVonna got rid of everything that belonged to Margot. She had given some things to various charities. She had either hidden or burned Margot's other belongings–the items she did not want the police to see– early on in her plan. She received two telephone calls regarding Margot's autopsy. It unnerved her to know that until the autopsy report had been finished and signed, the police could consider her an accomplice. She certainly did not want to arouse suspicion by trying to coax any details out of them.

JoVonna had to take time away from her companies and even from writing the proposal she had been working on because she still had not found anyone that she could tolerate to assume Margot's responsibilities. Being with the child all day and all night was a test for her nerves, and despite her efforts to cut back, she drank even more.

Michael George woke up at 6:30 a.m. on a Saturday morning. JoVonna tried to think of a way to make the baby shut up but her liquor-soaked brain knew only that she needed sleep, a lot more sleep. She fed him quickly and put him back in his bed without really opening her eyes. When

Michael George cried again less than an hour later because his stomach was upset, the sound cracked through the silence and echoed throughout the mansion. JoVonna was frustrated and tired and angry and hung over. She remembered that Margot had sometimes taken Michael George out for sun when he would cry incessantly. She stumbled out of the bed and gathered her son up and put him in his stroller. JoVonna pushed the stroller to the door leading the gardens. It was sunny, warm and windy and she decided that the elements could do a much better job of putting the child to sleep than she could, so she left the baby in his stroller in the gardens. The sound of birds chirping and the gentle breeze quieted the child and she decided to leave the door open a bit so she could listen for him. Instead, she passed out in her bed again and the liquor kept its stronghold on her for most of the day. While she slept, the child awakened, and when no one came to feed him, he cried himself back to sleep.

The skies clouded over and the winds picked up threefold. The top of the stroller was functioning like a sail, and soon the wheels started to move the stroller towards the steep, downward slope that led through the garden gate and down to her garages. The winds picked up more and it had started to rain now. The child was terrified. The stroller continued to travel downward over the grassy slopes. Every time the wind blew, the child was taken farther away from home. Almost an hour passed, and finally the big wheels on the stroller came to rest just next to the fence that separated JoVonna's property from the community within a community. The child was soaking wet and hungry and afraid. He cried again, but there was no one to hear him.

THE RAIN WILL TELL
Chapter Twenty-Five

JoVonna continued to sleep while almost everyone else in Richland Hills watched the rain slack up and started about their chores. Bessie, her husband Whistler, Willie Mae and several others in the separate community stood next to Whistler's station wagon. He was just about to start a job driving a truck for the City Of Richland Hills and he and Bessie were on their way to Greenspoint to share the good news with their family and friends. Bessie heard it first and dismissed it as the cries of a cat, but her maternal instincts quickly made her question what she heard. She told everyone to be quiet and allowed herself be led to where the cries were coming from. "One of you young folk climb up this here fence. I believes there be a child on the other side." Willie Mae's son easily scaled the wooden fence and yelled back over. "It be a baby all right, a white one. He in a stroller. He be soaked from head to toe, and he look kinda bad."

"Can you git the chile over here? We jus' can't leave him. Lawd knows how he got there." Bessie said. Willie Mae's son placed the child inside his T-shirt and tied a knot in the bottom of it. He used both hands to carefully climb back over the tall fence and handed the child to Bessie. She took a look at the pale, white baby and said to Whistler, "We got to git some hep for this here baby, else it goin' die." Bessie's oldest daughter ran to the house to find dry towels. Bessie took him inside and carefully dried his little head and his entire body.

"Git me some uh yo brother's pants and shirts to wrap 'round this here chile." When she finished dressing him, Bessie grabbed her purse off the counter and she and Whistler headed to the store to spend some of the money they had made selling vegetables that day to buy milk and diapers. Bessie held the frightened child to her bosom to calm him and threw a sweater over him to warm him.

"Now Bessie, you know we needs to git this chile to the police station soon as we kin get him fed. This here ain't good. That chile could have only come from one place and I don't know why or how, but I do know what it mean, and that is big trouble." Whistler leaned over and looked at his wife, and she nodded her head in agreement while she sang softly to the baby. Bessie handed the child to Whistler while she went in the store. A few minutes later they continued on in the direction of the police station and about two miles from the station, the car shook and sputtered and then stopped completely.

"You got gas, ain't you?"

"Yeah Bessie, I got gas. Jus' ain't quite put together 'nuf money for all the new parts I needs. I think I got somethin' in the back can fix it to tide us over tho'."

Michael George slept in Bessie's arms while Whistler got out to fix the station wagon.

JoVonna had finally awakened and was functioning in a haze as she fumbled for a cup of coffee. She took a pastry out of the container where Margot had always kept them and bit into it without even looking at it. She was surprised at how hard it was and dropped it on the counter. She had not looked at a clock and had no idea how long she had slept. When she remembered that she had left her son sleeping in the gardens, she went to the gardens to bring him in. She had left the window open and her kitchen floor was wet. When she stepped outside and saw the standing water, she realized just how much it had rained. When she did not see the stroller, she panicked. She went back into the mansion and made a drink to clear her head. She paced, kicking off her shoes and then putting them back on again. JoVonna went outside again and followed the muddy tire tracks from the stroller down the slopes of her property. She was out of breath when she got to the bottom and spotted the stroller. She pulled the top back and suddenly felt afraid.

JoVonna looked around and discovered the footprints near the fence.

"Dammit! She muttered to herself. *I know they took Michael George, but how did they know he was here?"*

She dragged the stroller back up the hill and hid it in her stables.

Crimson red nails drummed on the telephone stand outside her bedroom while she removed her muddy shoes and pondered how she would explain the fact that her child was missing to the police.

On the way to JoVonna's property to take the missing child report, one of the police officers drove past Whistler fixing the station wagon and saw Bessie sitting inside holding the white baby. The tires screeched on his patrol car as he backed up. Bessie and Whistler explained to him what happened. The officer confused the fear in the couple's eyes with guilt and arrested them.

Bessie tried to reason with the officer while her husband was being handcuffed.

"Offisuh, it happened jus' like my husband done told you."

The officer tightened the handcuffs on Whistler until he winced. Whistler raised his head but avoided direct eye contact with the officer. "Please Suh, don't put no handcuffs on my wife. She belong to the Motherboard at church and ain't caused nobody no harm."

Bessie was handcuffed too. The officer called in another patrol car to take Michael George to the hospital and JoVonna received a call from the police station notifying her that the child had been located. She was told to go to Richland Hills Hospital. She was also told that the suspects had been arrested. She felt a sigh of relief knowing that the situation would work to her advantage. JoVonna drove to the hospital to sign the necessary papers. The attending physician told JoVonna that it appeared the child was in the early stages respiratory distress and that it could turn into

143

double pneumonia. He also said the baby was suffering from mild shock. JoVonna knew that the situation regarding the child's health was grim, but her limited maternal instincts did not dictate that she should grieve or hold on to any particular emotion for long. JoVonna felt certain that the child was receiving the best care and that he would be well shortly. She spoke with the doctor again and left the hospital later that evening to go shower, think and drink. On the drive home, she reasoned that what those people in the community within the community had done this time would surely be all it would take to get them out of town. How dare they come onto her property and kidnap her child!

The next morning, JoVonna drove to what she still considered to be her land and approached a tree where Willie Mae and some of the other women sat reading to their children. She told them that Bessie and Whistler were in jail for stealing her baby. There was a still quietness. Even the children sat motionless, waiting for someone to explain to them what the news this white woman came bearing meant. Fear moved from Willie Mae's thoughts to her eyes. Bessie and Willie Mae had talked many times about the evil that lived up on that hill and now, here it was, standing right in front of them. JoVonna opened the case of money and documents that she brought with her and told them they needed to sell their homes to her. She said they would need the money to pay the legal costs for their friends. Two men who lived in the houses across the street approached the tree. JoVonna looked at the two large bodies that seemed to be made of black concrete and turned and quickly left. The fact that she knew nothing about these people still intimidated her.

Willie Mae put her hat on and went to town to call their attorney up north and tell him what had happened. Bessie and Whistler were still being held at the jail. They were terrified. They had been taken to separate interrogation rooms, and were being asked the same questions over and over again. Their attorney was involved in an on-going trial but had managed to get through to the prosecutor's office to see what the charges were. A few days later, just before Bessie and Whistler were to be arraigned, their attorney spoke with the Judge to submit a request that his clients be released on their own recognizance. He assured the Judge of their good standing in the community and said he would be in Richland Hills the next day. After the arraignment, the judge denied their attorney's request and the couple was told that they would soon be escorted back to their jail cells. Bessie cried on her husband's shoulder while they waited. They whispered softly to try and console each other. She told him that her heart ached for that child.

THE RAIN WILL TELL
Chapter Twenty-Six

The Chief of Police of Richland Hills sat his large body in the small rickety chair behind his desk. As he read through stacks of mail, he came across a letter in a plastic sleeve marked personal and confidential. He read the attached letter from the postal service:

Dear Postal Customer:

The enclosed letter was damaged in handling in the Postal Service. We realize that your mail is important to you and you have every right to expect it to be delivered intact and in good condition.....

He cut the taped, dirty envelope and began reading the thick handwritten letter inside. The letter was from Margot DuPrie. He looked at the postmark and then had his secretary bring him the DuPrie case file. The letter had been mailed just about a week before the incident at JoVonna Rossier's mansion where the dogs had killed Margot. He took another look at the letter the Post Office had attached explaining the damage and delay in delivering the letter. He shook his head.

"Damned Post Office! Rain or Shine, huh? How about On Time?"

He bit off the tip of his cigar and began reading. The contents caused him to upset his coffee cup without even realizing it. The letter explained that Margot planned to move out of the mansion shortly after she wrote it. She had written that she was afraid to stay much longer, that she knew too much and that her knowledge about JoVonna's business and personal life may be perceived as a threat to JoVonna. She told the Chief about the time JoVonna had cut her face with the fork and about the verbal assaults. Margot wrote that she felt JoVonna was capable of causing additional harm to her. Margot also wrote in the letter that she had kept notes on criminal activities that had taken place both at the mansion and at JoVonna's various businesses. The letter instructed the Chief to go to the butcher shop and ask Bill Henderson for the grocery orders that he had filled for JoVonna over the past several months. Margot explained in the letter that the notes were written in French on the back of the grocery orders that she had brought in to be filled for JoVonna. She said that she put the notes on the back of the grocery orders because she needed a way to document what was happening and feared if she wrote a letter to the Chief every time something happened, JoVonna might find one of the letters before she had a chance to mail it. Margot also said she suspected that JoVonna had been searching her room. The chief had someone from his office call the butcher shop to see if the grocery orders were still there. Bill Henderson answered the telephone and explained to the Chief just as he had explained to Margot that he kept all of Ms. Rossier's orders because she was very particular about her orders and complained often. The Chief sent one of his officers with a warrant to the butcher shop to confiscate the notes. He wiped the drops of coffee off of the binder that contained Margot DuPrie's file while pushing the intercom for his secretary.

"Yes Chief?"

"Get me the prosecutors office right away."

The Chief told the prosecutor about the letter he had received and together they revisited the Margot DuPrie case file. The butcher had the orders in a box ready to go when the officer arrived. He had seen the very small writing on the backside of some of the orders months earlier, but could not read French. He assumed they were cooking tips or some other scribble. Bill Henderson was asked to come to the police station for brief questioning and then released. The Chief made some calls, and later that afternoon, a tall, lanky officer from another local jurisdiction came to his office and translated the writing on the back of the orders one by one from French to English.

JoVonna stayed late at her office and at the end of the day, Shirley ran into her office with a telephone message saying that her Vice President, Timothy Wells had been admitted to the Hospital. He had gotten into a fight with his wife and she cut him several times with a straight razor. Mrs. Wells had been arrested. The message said that Timothy Wells' secretary would call again with more details. JoVonna raised her glass in a solitary cheer. Her plans to avenge Margot and Timothy were a success.

Shirley sat at her desk, wondering when JoVonna was going to get around to reading her letter of resignation. She had placed the envelope on her desk the day before, but JoVonna kept putting things on top of it. Shirley had been blessed with a new job and even if JoVonna did not read her letter, Shirley knew she would see this evil woman for the last time in just a few more days. She had brought in a brand new bottle of aspirin, put a bow on it and left it in her drawer for whoever was unfortunate enough to be JoVonna's new secretary.

At six o'clock the next morning, JoVonna was still muddled from sleep when she buzzed two squad cars through the main gate. They pulled to a halt on the circular drive directly in front of her mansion. While one officer served her the search warrant, the others fanned out, looking for the evidence Margot had written about. The Chief arrived and stood watching through horn-rimmed glasses. He bit off the tip off his cigar while the officers dug up the shallow grave of the young boy between the two oak trees outside JoVonna's guest bedroom. When the officer held up one of the small bones, the Chief spat and then cursed. JoVonna bit her lip to keep from smirking. She knew what evidence they were about to uncover because she had placed it there herself. When the officer finally lifted the sterling silver bracelet with the tip of his pencil, he cleaned away a small amount of mud and read aloud the inscription: Margot DuPrie.

JoVonna had prepared her alibi a long time ago. She was at a meeting the night that boy had been killed and buried in that shallow grave. Her name and ideas had been recorded as a part of the minutes of that meeting. The bracelet was, however, overwhelming evidence that Margot had been right there, in that hole. The law would have to prove that Margot, who could offer no defense from her grave, had not acted alone. JoVonna stood where the officers had surrounded her and watched as another officer removed notes and files from her mansion. She was nervous, but reasoned with herself that her accountants could justify any monetary discrepancies pertaining to her businesses and that a jury would understand about the notes and the actions she had taken against the families at the bottom of the hill. She had begun to relax just as two officers ran, out of breath, from the rear of the property. The officers and the Chief stood whispering in a semi-circle.

"Chief, we found something related to that arrest we made on that kidnapping charge. It happened just like that Bessie woman said. There are imprints from the wheels on that baby stroller from Ms. Rossier's gardens all the way down them slopes and clear over to where the fence divides the properties, and there are some tracks from the stroller being dragged back up the hill on only two wheels. We followed those tracks and found the beat up stroller locked in the old stables behind the mansion. And you know, if we'd had one of those good o'le Mississippi rains, those tracks would have been gone."

JoVonna was arrested. The prosecutor's office decided to charge her with felony child abandonment for Michael George while he reviewed the evidence to see if there was enough to charge her as an accomplice in the murder of the other little boy whose remains the sheriff's deputy found on her property. The Judge denied bail, partly because he knew the money meant nothing to her. His justification was that JoVonna had the resources and reason to leave town and never be seen again. Bessie and

Whistler's attorney came to tell them that the charges against them had been dropped and that they were free to go. The sound of the heavy door clanging behind them made Bessie jump.

Bessie put her head on her husband's shoulder as they left the jail. "Baby, I ain't never been mo' scared than I was while we was in that place. That place got the scent of somethin' mean." Whistler nodded his head in agreement. He looked at his wrists where the handcuffs had been and silently wished they had not been the ones who found the child. Bessie's heart was glad they had. Their attorney spent the next day talking to all of the families and then headed back to North Carolina.

Chapter Twenty-Seven

JoVonna's son lay in intensive care in the hospital. One of his tiny lungs had completely collapsed and he was being fed intravenously. Bessie and Whistler did not part issues much, but when it came to the subject of that little white baby lying there in the hospital, they disagreed. Bessie put the cornbread on the table while she told him about how her heart was telling her to go to the child and her arms wanted to hold him and let him know that life was not always so mean. Whistler agreed that the child needed love, but he also reminded her that finding that baby was the reason she had been in jail, and away from her own children.

It didn't take long for JoVonna to get into trouble behind the gray walls of the smoky, crowded jail. Her body craved alcohol and she was temperamental. She was condescending and disregarded the few inmates who tried to talk to her. She complained about the food, the uniforms and the showers. JoVonna claimed one of the inmates had head lice and refused to stand next to her in the shower line. She complained about how thin her mattress was and when she came back from taking her shower, the mattress was gone. Now she would have to sleep on the thin metal slats. Her status in Richland Hills meant nothing behind the walls of the jail. She learned that the hard way when her cellmate, a jet-black, muscular woman named Eunice, responded to JoVonna's degrading and condescending comment by slapping her hard across the face. She couldn't get the guards to do anything about it. Later that day, she found herself surrounded in the TV room. Clenched fists came from the crowd and swiftly and viciously attacked her. Unidentified feet kicked her and fingernails scratched her. When it was over, she found herself sitting on the floor, bruised and clutching her clothes to her bare breasts. She refused to cry. She did not want them to see how afraid she was. When the guards came and took her back to her cell, the inmates followed; some of them snickered, others outright howled in laughter until the guards told them to return to the TV room.

JoVonna sat on the bare cot in her cell and began to braid her hair. Almost a handful had been pulled out. She bit the inside of her lip to keep from crying. She had one of the best attorneys that money could retain and she was expecting a visit from her the next morning. JoVonna got out her pencil and paper and started making notes about the incident that happened earlier. At 9:00 a.m. the next morning, her attorney walked into the gray room with no windows and motioned for her client to sit at the table.

"JoVonna, I need details. My defense strategy is going to be partially that there was no malicious intent on your part, that this was just an accident. I think the prosecuting attorney is going to focus on the fact that you deliberately dragged that stroller back up to the stables and hid it."

JoVonna flinched.

"I'll have to find a way to either soften that fact or get around it. I'm going for a misdemeanor here, maybe probation."

JoVonna leaned forward and looked at her attorney through swollen and bloodshot eyes. "You go for whatever will get me out of this hellhole right now!"

The attorney nodded to acknowledge her client's demand.

"I will address the issue of the grave found on your property as soon as I hear where the Chief of Police and the Prosecutor's office are going with it." She hesitated, tilting her head slightly and looked at her client. "Just how did that little black boy come to be buried on your property?" She looked around and quickly threw her hands up to silence JoVonna. "No, no, don't answer that now. We'll address that issue when we have to. Right now, let's concentrate on your child." She pushed up her sleeves, revealing a diamond bracelet equally as elegant as the rings she wore. The lawyer reached into her briefcase for a pen and began writing notes and key words. She tossed another pad to JoVonna and asked her to quickly note what she remembered. They talked softly a few minutes longer and then JoVonna was returned to her cell where her cellmate sat holding her slippers and glaring at her.

"Keep your shit on your side of the cell!" JoVonna's cellmate's voice was quite, yet cold and commanding.

JoVonna learned very quickly that in jail, you have to defend yourself, no matter how afraid you are. She braced herself for another territorial argument with her cellmate about where she had the right to leave her belongings within the very limited confines of the cell.

Eunice threw the slippers across the room and they landed in JoVonna's bunk. JoVonna looked at the woman over the rim of the book she was reading. Eunice snatched the book away from her and tore it up. She took JoVonna's blanket and dared her to take it back. JoVonna put Eunice's pillow in the toilet. The jet-black woman looked down at her and told her in an even, almost whispered tone that she was just another faded green uniform now. Eunice also promised JoVonna that when she felt like it, she was going to kill her. JoVonna sat on the edge of her bare cot and watched Eunice drift off to sleep.

JoVonna decided she needed to find a way to spread some cash around in the jail. She already knew whom she needed to call when she got her next telephone privileges. In the next few days, the guards began receiving very expensive, anonymous gifts delivered from various department stores. She used a piece of her monogrammed stationery to write a note that simply said, "more to come" and dropped it outside her cell just before bed check. Two days later, she sat on her cot. The mattress had mysteriously returned. She thought about what had just happened and folded her arms across her chest in satisfaction. It was amazing just how much her money could buy for her. Now that she had managed to get some of her money circulating within the confines of the jail, she found herself being escorted by a guard every morning and again every afternoon to a room marked Employees Only. She was allowed to drink imported liquor and a jar of olives rested on the top shelf of a metal locker. When she went out for recreation, several inmates were sitting at a table looking at newspaper clippings about her. The effect of their stares was like walking into a brick wall. She could not escape their cold eyes.

THE RAIN WILL TELL
Chapter Twenty-Eight

Bessie and Whistler had been going to the hospital almost every night since they had been released from jail. The duty nurse flatly refused to let them see the child at first, since they were obviously not relatives.

"Why are you here?" she asked, giving her paperwork more attention than them.

"We's jus' concerned, is all."

Bessie stiffened with indignation as her husband nodded his head to affirm his wife's statement. They persisted and finally Nurse Brenda Billford saw them one night. After she helped Marcus prove the child was not his, she had continued to follow the stories in the newspaper regarding JoVonna and her child and saw no harm in letting them see the baby. They stood just inside the open doorway. Bessie cooed and sang softly to the baby. In the passing days, Bessie and her husband brought a teddy bear for the child. Bessie was allowed to hold the baby and to try to get him to eat again. Michael George was almost six months old and his doctor had noted a concern about his weight on his chart. The nurses got to know Bessie and Whistler and eventually encouraged their visits. No one else came to see Michael George, and they felt that the despondent child might respond to the couple's nurturing. The following Monday, Bessie stopped at the nurses' station and spoke to everyone. She left a warm pineapple upside down cake on the counter and walked down the hall to Michael George's room. She took off her old hat and placed it on the nightstand next to where the child lay in a fitful sleep.

Bessie knew something was wrong the minute she saw the child. She picked the baby up. He was pale and still now, as he looked at her with eyes that seemed to summarize his life. Bessie sat there engulfed by tears, watching the desperately ill child. He reached up and touched her face. She watched him try to hold on to his smile. He closed his eyes and did not open them again. Bessie clutched the child tighter to her bosom and ran down to the nurses' station. He had used the last of his strength and went limp in her arms just as she handed him over to the nurse. Doctors worked on the boy for hours, but he was pronounced dead before the night was over.

One of the guards shined a flashlight in JoVonna's cell and told her she had an emergency telephone call. The news kept her awake the rest of the night. The next morning, she still could not identify all of the different emotions she felt. At nine o'clock, JoVonna's attorney was anxiously waiting for her client to be escorted into the tiny room where she would discuss a new strategy.

"You know that the death of your son means the prosecutor is going for murder now. He is going to tell the jury that you never called the hospital to check on your son. You are not on record here as requesting to see your son, even once. We have got to come up with some damned good explanations or the jury is going to put you away for the rest of your life."

"What should I do?" JoVonna tapped her brittle nails on the table. She needed a drink.

"For God sakes, call to make some burial arrangements! Then get on the telephone and call some alcohol treatment centers. Tell whoever answers the phone that you called once before when you first got arrested. Tell them that you were told that they would handle the paperwork for getting you treated while you are in jail. Then tell them that you are following up because you haven't heard anything. Make sure they write down your name and that you get theirs."

JoVonna wrote furiously on both sides of the sheet of paper in front of her.

"Maybe we can convince a jury that you were consumed with trying to get treatment for your illness and that's why you couldn't see your son. Otherwise, the jury will see you as cold, uncaring and ruthless, with no maternal instincts. I requested a copy of the child's hospital records. I found the report that supports your claim that your son had difficulty breathing at birth and that he used a respirator and needed occasional breathing treatments. I still don't know if it would be effective to have you testify about Michael George's problems when he was born. On the one hand, the jury may be sympathetic. On the other hand, they may hate you even more for knowing that the child had problems and not taking better care of him. Write down everything that happened right after you delivered your son."

JoVonna's hand froze as if a clamp had suddenly been placed on her wrist. She looked away from her attorney.

"I don't know........I don't remember much. I mean, I remember reading his records."

"Dammit, JoVonna, don't you remember seeing your own son being treated?"

JoVonna didn't answer. The silence was broken when her attorney's pen smashed against the wall. She spoke through clenched teeth.

"I am going to try to convince the jury that the child's lungs were already weak and that double pneumonia is not necessarily the result of his exposure to that damned storm. We have got a lot of trouble here. Let's hope the prosecution doesn't object me right out of the courtroom. I'll see you for your arraignment on Friday."

Later in the day, JoVonna was escorted up to the room where she drank. One of the guards, a tall wiry man with sharp features sat casually on the windowsill. The other guard, who was handsome and had a good physique, sat in a chair with his feet propped up on a small wooden table. The taller of the two men blew out a cloud of smoke. Both men listened and looked at each other, sending signals with their eyes while JoVonna rattled on about things that her inmates had done, in hopes of getting better protection for herself and staying in good favor with the guards. The conversation and the liquor also distracted her from her own problems.

Friday morning started out as a dark, gray day. The town awakened to unceasing rain and loud claps of thunder; the kind that had frightened Bessie's children into bed with her. They watched with wide-eyed pride as their father checked his new uniform in the mirror and put on his hat. Bessie put away the breakfast food and kissed him goodbye. She watched as he made his way to the station wagon. Whistler would meet up with the other drivers and they would be briefed on their routes. Later he would start his first day as a truck driver for the largest grocery store in Richland Hills.

Attorneys waited in a small hallway at the prosecutor's office to file briefs, obtain information or pick up documents. JoVonna's attorney was amongst them and cursed herself for not sending her clerk to pick up the file copies the prosecutor's office had left for her at the last minute. She thought that if she picked them up herself she could use the extra few minutes to go over them. JoVonna's arraignment was in forty-five minutes. She took the files from the impatient woman on the other side of the window and pushed them into her briefcase. She pulled her hat down as far as it would go and pulled the collar of her raincoat up to meet it. She stood in front of the revolving door, watching time escape her while she waited a minute, hoping for a break in the blinding rain.

Whistler checked his schedule one final time and then drove the large truck away from the parking lot. He followed his checklist completely and then took off, following the directions to his first delivery.

JoVonna's attorney checked her watch again. It had been raining very lightly when she left and she had opted to leave her car at the courthouse and now regretted having to run the two blocks back over there. She pulled her hat down even further and opened the huge umbrella that had no chance of keeping her dry. The light turned red as she crossed the corner of Beaumont and Adair. She jumped in and out of puddles for the next block and stepped out into the street to cross Winchester Avenue. Whistler saw the sudden movement through the sheets of rain that overpowered his windshield wipers and immediately tried to stop. The truck skidded and then slammed into the attorney, killing her instantly and sending her briefcase sailing across the street. Papers were strewn everywhere. The rain was washing away JoVonna's chance at freedom. Whistler dispatched the accident on his truck radio and was at the attorney's side now, shielding her with his raincoat. His tears were hidden in the rain.

The siren on the ambulance pierced through the sound of the steady rain and the red lights blinked frantically against the dark gray sky. The Judge, the Grand Jury, the prosecuting attorney and JoVonna were all watching the big round clock at the back of the courtroom. One hour later, the Judge was made aware of the accident and the attorney's death. JoVonna was already back in her cell when she got the news about her attorney, and she felt as if someone had submerged her in ice cold water. She would have to hire a new attorney and start all over with a new strategy. She wanted a drink now. Her lips felt like sandpaper and she suffered from cold sweats. It was still a couple of hours before the guard would come to take her to drink. JoVonna's cellmate had been watching her since she returned from the courthouse. "Why you back so damn soon? I thought that uppity-ass lawyer of yours was going to get you out of here."

"She died."

"What?"

"My attorney died in an accident this morning." Even as she said the words, JoVonna still could not believe that her attorney was dead.

Eunice sucked her teeth and rolled over on her stomach.

Whistler had stayed at the scene of the accident until the police finished taking his statement and preserving the scene as best they could in the steady rain. He went home and told his family the terrible news. "I sho' am sorry she died. Lawd knows, I didn't mean to hit huh." Bessie stood behind her husband and rubbed his shoulders while he finished telling them what happened that morning.

"I didn't see huh comin'. When that windshield wiper moved out of the way, there she was."

THE RAIN WILL TELL
Chapter Twenty-Nine

Mother Nature provided a perfect day for Marcus and Lilly's garden wedding. Glen Boyd's lawn had been meticulously cared for. They had invited nearly the entire town, and today they would see their carefully laid plans carried out. Early in their planning stages, they decided that they would move to Decatur, Georgia immediately after they were married. The scandals of Richland Hills had left them with too many bad memories and JoVonna had seen to it that they would practically have to restart Lilly's printing business from scratch. They pooled the money from the sale of their homes and bought a property with peach trees and a small pond on a five-acre lot in Georgia. The couple leased a building and made arrangements for the printing equipment to be sent ahead. Marcus was in the process of buying part ownership of a small business in downtown Decatur.

The townsfolk beamed as they watched Lilly and Marcus prepare to get married. The florist had placed pink and white roses along the carpeted path where Lilly walked. The couple stood on a platform that had been built for the occasion, and the train of Lilly's wedding gown cascaded down the steps. Huge vases of long-stemmed pink and white roses formed a semi-circle around the couple. Two small white candles burned next to a larger white candle that would be lit to symbolize their unity. Timers had been set to light the walkways at dusk, and the trees had been decorated with tiny white bulbs that would glow like showers of light against the dark sky. Lilly cried, as she stood there in her antique white wedding gown and exchanged vows with her handsome, tuxedo-clad husband. The ceremony was beautiful and when it was over, the bride and groom changed clothes and rejoined their guests in a combination reception and goodbye party. Marcus and Lilly cut the cake and champagne flowed as toast after toast was made. The aroma of southern barbecue, succulent roasted chicken, Cornish hens and other expertly prepared foods floated into the late summer air. Several couples danced on the lush, green lawn and others gathered in groups of chairs around white tables containing large vases of pink and white Gladiolas with bows and trailing ribbons that had been meticulously arranged. Marcus made his way slowly through friends that wanted to wish him and his new bride well towards the gazebo where Lilly sipped champagne and retold the story of how Marcus had proposed with the ring in the cup. They enjoyed the crowd and laughed and reminisced.

Councilman Glen Boyd stepped into the gazebo and took a seat next to Marcus and Lilly. "It's been a long time since the whole town has been this happy, and we all know the reason." he said, as he flicked a blade of grass off of his newly polished shoes. Marcus and Lilly looked at each other.

"JoVonna hasn't been around stirring up evil like she usually does. I believe she deserves worse than sitting over there in jail."

"Why do you feel so strongly about it?" Lilly asked.

"Marcus never told you?"

Lilly looked at Marcus. Her eyes were question marks.

"My problems with JoVonna started long before I had the pleasure of meeting you, Lilly. JoVonna has done so many things to so many people that I try not to cloud my mind with them."

"I know what you mean," Lilly said. "I have a few newspaper articles that I saved about some of the situations and scandals JoVonna has been involved in."

"It's more like a scrapbook, and I think it has turned my new bride here, into quite the detective." Marcus teased.

"Well, as far as I am concerned, JoVonna has had free sovereignty in this town for long enough. I am glad that she is in jail and I hope that someday, someone will find a way to put a stop to her evil ways forever." Lilly said. She finished the last spoonful of food on her plate. "Glen, what kind of problem did you have with JoVonna?" Lilly asked.

Glen leaned forward and wiped the perspiration from his forehead with a white handkerchief. "Lilly, I owned a very profitable liquor store. JoVonna bought liquor for all of her big parties as well as her personal stock there. On the occasion of one of her rather large parties, my new deliveryman forgot to deliver the liquor to her mansion. She came tearing into the store, demanding that I fire him because she had to cancel the dinner party at the last minute. She claimed that she lost out on a deal that could have potentially been worth millions and that she was humiliated when she had to cancel the dinner party. I knew what the deliveryman had done was bad for my business and that I would probably have to let him go, but she wanted the satisfaction of watching me fire him right then and there. I knew how badly he needed the job, so I refused, and we stood there having words until I cursed at her and told her to get the hell out of my store. She threatened me.

To make a long story short, JoVonna knew that I would be at a city council meeting when she sent an under-aged guy over to my store to buy some whiskey. My clerk said the customer looked to be of age. He did not check his identification closely enough. JoVonna filed a complaint with the Bureau of Alcohol and Tobacco. All I could say in my defense was that my clerk said the customer looked to be way over twenty-one. My liquor license was revoked. Before I could do anything about it, all of our savings were gone and we lost our house. My wife was carrying our third child. Marcus took my family and me into his home, fed us, clothed us and let us stay there for free.

When I managed to save enough money, I bought a piece of land. A lot of people pitched in to help me build a fine house on that land. JoVonna went searching around down at City Hall and found that I did not have clear title. The legal description said that my land overlapped some land that her daddy had given her by a couple of inches. While the whole mess was in litigation, my house was mysteriously set on fire and what was left had to be bulldozed. I thought for sure JoVonna would go to jail for that, but like everything else she has done, no one could prove she was responsible. Well, my wife miscarried, and there we went back to live with Marcus."

"I am sorry that JoVonna caused so much hardship to your family." Lilly said.

"I am just glad that Marcus was such a good friend." Glen replied.

Lilly patted her husband's hand tenderly. She looked at Glen's beautiful home and property again and sighed with contentment.

"Marcus and I thank you again for letting us have our wedding here. You certainly have a beautiful home now. It looks like you finally got what you deserved." She wondered again how Glen could afford such a large and expensive home.

Glen's smile was wicked as he nodded at Lilly. Marcus excused himself to get drinks and Lilly and Glen sat a few moments longer and continued to talk. A few minutes later, he told Lilly that he needed to take care of a matter inside his house and excused himself. When Marcus returned, he told Lilly that he had not realized that Glen still harbored so much hatred for JoVonna. Someone asked the bride for a dance before they could talk any more.

The guards had broken up several fights between JoVonna and her cellmate during the course of their confinement. Their most recent altercation was so serious that her cellmate had served several days in solitary confinement. On the day she was returned to her cell, Eunice waited for the guards to leave and hit JoVonna in the mouth with her fist. JoVonna got up off the cold floor and lunged out, raking her nails across Eunice's face. She touched her face and looked at the blood on her hand.

Eunice renewed the threat she had made to JoVonna previously.

"You will not walk out of this jail alive."

JoVonna did not answer, but knew she had to find a way to expedite the request she had submitted to her attorney to be moved to another cell. Eunice had paid the guards a premium to cut off JoVonna's liquor supply for a few days. The guards figured that if JoVonna went without alcohol for a while that she would be willing to pay them even more than she paid now for the privilege of drinking, so they agreed to cut her off. Days had passed since her last drink, and each day, JoVonna hoped that the guards would come and take her to the room marked Employees Only, but they did not, nor did they offer any explanation. She sat in the recreation room frustrated, with sweaty palms, watching the guards who used to drink with her openly flirting with the inmates while they played cards and watched television. Women took turns braiding each other's hair.

One of the women looked at the large clock on the wall and then pulled out a sketchpad and said she wanted to do a drawing of the guard. The other women quickly distracted him by touching what they considered were his assets and pointing them out to the artist. A tall, slender, inmate with a pock scarred face and stringy brown hair that was pulled tightly into a ponytail slowly stepped away from the excitement and rounded the corner. She picked up a small bottle of gin that had been carefully hidden earlier. She gargled with it and went back around the corner where she stood close enough for JoVonna to smell the alcohol and motioned for her to come and have a drink with her.

JoVonna was like a cat drawn to milk as she walked away from the guard and the other inmates. The woman led JoVonna to the kitchen where they had two quick drinks. They joked about how easy it was to get anything they wanted inside the jail, and when JoVonna opened her mouth to laugh, her cellmate stepped out of the darkness to follow up on the threat she had made earlier. She stuffed a towel into JoVonna's mouth and taped it shut. The two women forced the silent but resistant JoVonna up to the sixth floor. Eunice stayed with her while the other inmate rinsed out her mouth, tossed in a handful of mints and went to rejoin the crowd and make sure the guard saw her. She signaled to a stout, blonde inmate who was leaning against the wall watching the guard. While the women tried to coax the guard into taking off his shirt for the portrait, the blonde woman slipped away just as easily as the inmate who had just returned. She stubbed out her cigarette and went to the sixth floor where JoVonna sat on the floor with her eyes bulging from fear. Eunice's jet-black physique was camouflaged as she stood in the darkness behind JoVonna. She used a small flashlight to secure the knotted sheets that she was tying around the column next to the window. Both women worked quickly to complete their roles in the plan. The blonde woman gathered up the crowbar that had been used to open the window, the tape, and the other items. She looked around the room to make sure that nothing was left behind. Then she closed the door and stood outside, ready to distract anyone who might happen along.

Lilly and Marcus finished loading their wedding gifts in their car. They went back to say goodbye to all of their guests one last time. They stood holding hands, looking at how beautiful their wedding had been. The song the musicians played trailed off as they were walking across the lawn, headed to their car. It had started to rain slightly, and Marcus said out loud exactly what his bride was thinking. "Oh well, at least it didn't rain during the wedding." Councilman Glen Boyd walked up to Lilly as she got into the car and handed her a small leather notebook tied with a ribbon and a bow. He wished the couple well, smiled and walked away. Once they were out on the highway, Lilly remembered the gift she had put in her purse. She took the ribbon and bow off and turned on the interior light and began to look through it. The notebook contained poems and short

stories written in Calligraphy by Glen Boyd. One of the
pages was dog-eared. Lilly began reading:

*When the storms and turbulence and wicked nights loomed
stagnant and threatened the strength of the Lilly,*

*The moment was opportune, the vengeance
Masqueraded.*

*Then I commanded that storm to slumber and
brought forth the long quiet after the storm.*

*And after the quiet, the storm would re-gather
itself, propelled by the blind winds of uncertainty, and form
a union for strength in revelation; extending its power to
the slivers of light, now turned dim.*

*I severed that union and left it in still darkness.
And the storm lost its course and drifted for a time,
Slowly dissipating into nothing.*

Lilly read the poem again, more slowly this time,
trying to figure out why Councilman Boyd gave it to them
and what significance it held.

"My God, this is a metaphor!" she said as she read it
yet again. That is why he dog-eared this poem. He wanted
to make sure we read this one.

Her heart quickened. Suddenly she was pale and felt
faint.

"What's the matter?" Marcus asked, concerned.

"Glen did it! He paid JoVonna back for what she did
to his family. He also took revenge for what JoVonna did to
us. Glen has used his poetry to secretly tell us that he repaid
you for being so kind to his family when JoVonna did all of

those horrible things to them. He just gave us his confession as a wedding gift."

"What on earth are you talking about?" Marcus frowned.

"Pull over and read this."

When Marcus stopped the car, he and Lilly sat in the dim car light unraveling the mysterious poem.

Lilly pointed to the first lines as they read together.

"When JoVonna pulled that stunt at your banquet, she threatened your political career. I think that's what Glen is writing about when he says - *threatens the strength of the Lilly*. He is talking about you."

"*The vengeance masqueraded, the moment opportune*" says exactly what we talked about earlier this evening, about JoVonna having done so many things to so many people that everyone wished that someone else would stop her. No one would have associated what is happening to her now with what happened to Glen's family years ago.

"Marcus, I think Glen had something to do with JoVonna being drugged that night, and if she was raped after she was drunk or drugged, then that would explain why she didn't know who the father of the child was."

"But the police never found any evidence." Marcus looked at his wife and then back at the poem.

"True, but no one ever even thought to question Glen. There were no clues that led to him. He was at the banquet, but he could have arranged for someone else to do it. The police investigation was focused on you because JoVonna told everyone that you drugged and impregnated her, but we proved to the entire town that she was wrong. When the police couldn't find any evidence, the case must have gone to a cold case file.

"JoVonna is "*the storm*", and "*the quiet after the storm*" is the coma she lapsed into." Marcus shook his head in amazement at his new bride.

"You have become quite the detective on this case, haven't you?"

Lilly wanted Marcus to focus his undivided attention on what she was saying.

"Marcus, would you please just listen to me?"

"Okay. I am listening."

"When we were talking in the gazebo, Glen told me that he knew JoVonna had gotten information about your joint venture partnership and that she had manipulated the deal. She was also the one who caused all the problems for me when I moved my printing business into that new building. I don't know how he knew all of those things. It's like someone either intentionally or unintentionally told him everything. He knew explicit details, Marcus."

"Remember when JoVonna was tearing the town apart looking for clues and you told me she brought that suitcase full of cash to the council meeting? Well, I think that's what Glen means when he says, "**to extend power**" which in this case is money, "*to form a union for revelation*." She was looking to pay someone on the City Council for answers. Don't you see, Marcus? When she offered the money, Henry Talbert must have agreed to sell information to her. Glen found out about it and killed Henry before he could tell her anything. That's why the police found him in that bank with that sign pinned to his chest saying "No News Today."

"Speaking of money, where do you suppose Glen Boyd got the money to pay for that exquisite new home?" Lilly asked. I bet Glen found a way to get a large sum of money from JoVonna while he was planning this whole thing out. Remember that newspaper article that said JoVonna filed a police report because she was missing some documents and a large sum of money?

Marcus looked closely at the poem again, and this time it was he who associated the next clue in the poem with what really happened.

"Then, that's what he means when he says- "*severed the union and left it in darkness*." He took away the opportunity for JoVonna to meet with Henry by somehow luring him to that abandoned bank and killing him. And what has become of that whole investigation while JoVonna sits in jail?" "*It has dissipated into nothing*."

"Marcus, do you think we should go to the police?"

"Are you kidding? They would probably throw us in jail for misinterpreting poetry. We need something more solid."

Lilly leaned over and looked him squarely in the face.

"Marcus, you know as well as I do that with everything Glen said to us in his gazebo, that he intended for us to put two and two together. We know what happened now. Glen Boyd was behind everything that happened to JoVonna."

"I just think it would have been very difficult for Glen to pull something like that off and still be so visible at the banquet. He danced, he talked, he ate; we saw him quite a bit that evening." Marcus said.

"There were hundreds of people at that banquet. Some people came early and some left early. Glen could have slipped out before the police arrived or, he could have hired someone to carry out his plans." Lilly looked at the poem again. "JoVonna is still sitting back there in jail wondering who was responsible for the things that happened to her on the night of the banquet. If we go to the police, the whole story could be made public and then she will know too. I think Glen wants JoVonna to know he did it. Even if it means he would have to be investigated. After all, the police haven't found any evidence. Glen could walk away a free man and for once in her life, JoVonna couldn't do a damned thing about it." Lilly was still holding the book of poetry in her lap. "So, do you still think we should wait and reconsider this before saying anything?"

"Yes, I do." Marcus replied. "After all, on the surface, it's only a poem. Who knew how long it would take us to get around to reading it?"

"If she were not sitting over there in jail right now, I am sure that JoVonna would have done something to try to sabotage our wedding today." Lilly leaned over and kissed her new husband on the cheek.

"JoVonna has been a woman whose evil intentions were fueled by alcohol for a long time. She has been turning this entire town upside down since the day those families moved in from Greenspoint. If it had not been for Glen and what this poem says he did, I might not have been re-elected as mayor." Marcus said.

Lilly and Marcus continued on in silence. Neither of them realized the irony that life and death sometimes seems to occupy the same time frame.

Lilly was unaware that the reason she could no longer tolerate the smell of Marcus' pipe tobacco was the newly conceived life inside of her.

At the same time, the nails that secured the window shut had been pried out and the knotted sheets had been lowered out of the window to make it appear as if JoVonna had attempted to escape from jail. Eunice pulled off the tape that had bound JoVonna's hands and mouth and removed the towel. JoVonna knew that her life was in danger. She reached out and violently struck Eunice across the face, hoping to distract her long enough to escape. Eunice hit JoVonna squarely in the face with her fist. Her legs felt wobbly, and she fell back onto a chair. JoVonna picked up the chair and hit Eunice in the face. Eunice spat out blood and teeth. She shook her head and held on to the table to steady herself. JoVonna ran towards the door. Eunice reached out and grabbed her by her long braid. A vicious backhanded slap sent JoVonna flying into the wall. She felt her nose start to bleed as she slid down the wall. Eunice grabbed her legs and pulled her across the floor by her feet.

She kicked JoVonna in her stomach and pulled her up to the window.

JoVonna kicked frantically and used her fingernails to claw into Eunice's wrists. Eunice hit JoVonna in the face several more times. Her head jerked backwards with each blow. Desperation was stretched across JoVonna's brow.

"Please don't do this. I can get you out of here!" JoVonna screamed into Eunice's face.

"Bitch, you couldn't even get yourself out, but everyone is going to think you died trying."

Eunice laughed into the rainstorm and pushed JoVonna from the sixth-floor window. JoVonna's screams were muted by the wind and rain. She laid on the ground now, her face and body pierced by the unyielding and imposing barbed-wire fence. The rain washed away her substance, her strength, her power and her blood. With her parents already dead, her lifeline had been severed and was being washed away by the Mississippi rain.

THE END

Inquire about how to purchase additional copies
of this novel at:
luv2write4u@sbcglobal.net